Daughters

Of

Deliverance

A TIME TO LOVE

A. Michele Henderson

Aunt Elnora,
Thank you for all your prayers and support! ♡
Love You Much
— Andrea
7-26-16

Ardena Henderson Publishing ©2016 2nd Edition

amichelehenderson.com

Table of Contents

Acknowledgments

I give all honor to my Heavenly Father for allowing me through His Spirit to collide with my identity in Christ. To my husband James T. Henderson for your abiding love, unwavering support and commitment to our union; we share something so rare in this hour and I am honored to be your wife. To our son Joshua for bringing an abundance of love and joy into our lives, Mommy loves you so much it hurts! To my mother for all your support and encouragement, I love and appreciate you. To my cousin Phryne for daring me to live my dream and for being my advocate, I love you. To my besties and sisters who always show up on my behalf and encourage me through it all, you ladies rock! To my pastor Dr. Karen S. Bethea for a solid foundation in God's Word, I honor and thank you. To my family, in-loves and mentors for your prayers and support, I love and appreciate you all.

Chapter 1: Truth Be Told

Apple shook violently as tears fell across her ebony cheeks and into her ears. After seven months of therapy Dr. Washington had finally reached the root of Apple's pain and dysfunction. As she laid on the sky blue leather couch she couldn't believe she had told someone. She was only 9 when her older brother told her to lay on the basement floor. Chester Brown was 13 years old when he began to violate his baby sister. By the time she was 11 he had included his best friend Carl in her abuse. When she was 12 and Chester and Carl were 16 Mrs. Brown caught the three of them when she came home early from work. She told the boys to leave and scolded Apple for being fast. Apple told Mrs. Brown it had gone on since she was 9 and Mrs. Brown told her to forget about it because she probably did something to cause it. A few months after being caught, Apple was taken to get her first abortion. The possibility of being pregnant by her own brother was never discussed or dealt with. By the time she was 13 Apple had a reputation. She had been teased for so long by other girls because of her ebony skin, full lips and un-kept hair that she had finally found a way to feel accepted. The boys told her they loved her. She saw nothing wrong with boys passing her off to their friends since Chester had given her to Carl. Shortly after her first abortion she became pregnant with her first daughter. Thus began the cycle of promiscuity, abortions, out of wedlock children and sexually transmitted diseases.

Dr. Washington knew that Apple's therapy had only just begun and decided to see her once per week pro bono because her insurance didn't cover the kind of help she would need. Zola Washington decided that Apple was her opportunity to give back.

For the first time in her life Apple felt free. Her secret had become too heavy to carry. She knew Mrs. Brown saw her as a failure and blamed her for what happened. Even after Chester was arrested for rape at 17, Mrs. Brown blamed the victim. He had gotten away with it because the young lady dropped the charges when her promiscuity came in to question. Over the next few years, incidents of sexual assaults followed Chester with no justice. At the age of 21, Chester raped a suburban girl without a sexual history and finally was convicted and sentenced to 9 years in prison. Mrs. Brown never acknowledged his wrong doing and took the stand as a character witness during the trial testifying under oath that Chester had no past of sexual misconduct. What Mrs. Brown didn't realize was that her sworn testimony left Apple numb, rejected and shattered. What Apple didn't realize was that she was next in line for restoration.

Meanwhile across town, The Hairstons' and the Evans' conspired to surprise Ryan and Blake with a third anniversary family cruise. It was only April so they had six months to plan the trip without it taking away from Alexis and Paris's June wedding and Nia and Devin's August wedding. Ryan and Blake labored so hard in ministry and their parents knew it was time for a break. Their church had started in a movie theater with 16 members and had grown to a storefront with over 200 members and now in two and a half years they bought and converted a call center into a 750 seat sanctuary with offices, a nursery, café/bookstore and media center with 3 services and 800 members. Ryan holds services on Saturday night at 6pm and Sunday mornings at 7am and 10am. Bible studies are church wide and held on Tuesday nights. The church has a strong intercessory mantle with great community involvement. Without trying, men account for 40 percent of the church's members and marriages account for three quarters of the adult congregation. The church is known for building strong families and has seen its share of restored marriages and child/parental relationships. God's Love Church or GLC was indeed a special place.

Blake was full of joy as she and Aunt Vivian watched Alexis beam at her final alteration appointment. Lexi was so busy that she had lost another seven pounds since her last alteration. Her golden complexion glowed without makeup and her ebony hair rested just above her waist thanks to a weekly press for the last 10 years. Her trumpet style dress fell into a cascade of tulle. Lexi will wear an emerald green sash to compliment the emerald green printed dresses of her bridesmaids and the solid emerald green dress of her matron of honor and cousin, Blake. Blake will be escorted by Paris's best friend Coby and Ryan will officiate the service. The wedding and reception will take place on the Lovehall estate in Hampton, Virginia. Blake couldn't be happier to see all the people she loved to have love of their own. How did they all become so blessed, she quizzed. Later in the summer she and Ryan would be matron of honor and best man in Nia and Devin's wedding. She was going to miss her bestie who would move to Chicago with her new husband. Sitting in the bridal shop allowed Blake to feel like everything was perfect; little did she know a storm was headed her way.

Ryan was reclining in his man cave when he received a call from Prophet Tevin. After exchanging jokes and chuckles Tevin invited Ryan to preach at his annual men's conference during July in Dallas, Texas. Ryan accepted after looking through his calendar and itinerary. Ryan and Prophet Tevin had become good friends since the revival in South Carolina where he and Blake first mistook him for Joelle's ex. When he stepped out onto the platform he did resemble the other Tevin Coleman from the back, while he greeted the Elders sitting in the pulpit. It wasn't until he turned around to face the crowd at least 10 seconds after being announced that a sigh of relief came over Ryan and Blake's faces. Months later a true friendship had formed between Ryan and Prophet Tevin or PT as he was affectionately called and Blake and his wife Gabrielle. Tevin and Gabrielle Coleman live in

Atlanta, Georgia and are the parents of three year old twins Tiffany and Timothy. Each year Tevin hosts a men's conference in a different major city. His prophetic mantle was second to none and he was known for integrity and accuracy. Before ending their conversation PT told Ryan that he would enter a season of brokenness but to be encouraged because God will not only restore him but repay him for his faithfulness. Ryan received the word of the Lord but wondered what kind of trial he would have to be faithful through.

It was almost 80 degrees on an April evening in Dallas, when Brooke Taylor slid into her automobile. She inhaled the scent of leather and the cotton candy air freshener clipped onto the dashboard vent. Brooke started the engine to bask in the cool breeze of the air conditioner. She closed her eyes in an attempt to have a moment to herself. Once her skin cooled down she recognized the smell of the Joe Malone fragrance she'd put on over 12 hours ago. As the owner of an upscale shoe boutique in Highland Park, Brooke was no stranger to long hours and sore muscles. The long hours on her feet and heavy lifting were countered by a weekly pedicure and massage. Brooke's business was so successful that she often made house calls after hours and hosted stiletto parties for the elite. Brooke found her niche while at Wilberforce in her native Ohio. She noticed that even broke college students were willing to spend school refund money on high end bags and shoes. Since the high end handbag market was exclusive to brand boutiques and department stores,

Brooke chose shoes. With a shoe boutique, trade laws allowed her to sell a variety of high end designer shoes within the same store. Brooke moved to Dallas with her grandmother after becoming pregnant in undergrad. Just days after winter break, her boyfriend broke up with her to be with his high school sweetheart. Brooke had found out during holiday break that she was pregnant but decided to tell her boyfriend in person when spring semester began. Unfortunately her son's father broke up with her over the phone and would never meet with her privately. It was then that Brooke decided to move to Dallas and raise her son without his father knowing he existed. Later that year on August 17th Brooke gave birth to her son Bradley Michael Taylor on a scorching Texas afternoon. Bradley was now 5 years old and had just finished his first year of kindergarten. Brooke's Granny Mae takes care of Brad while Brooke is working and while she attends school. With Granny Mae's help, Brooke has already received her bachelor's degree in accounting and is now a semester away from a master's degree in business administration. Brooke has paid off Granny Mae's house, mortgages a house for herself, bought a Porsche in cash and pays tuition for her and Bradley all because of shoes. Her clients buy so many pairs that Brooke often turns a ten thousand dollar profit each week. Dallas was a great market since sports teams and oil tycoons afforded her clients the ability to shop freely. In addition to the Dallas/Fort Worth area, word of mouth has created business for Brooke all over the country. She often ships shoes to new clients and has done stiletto parties in Miami, Atlanta, Orange County and Seattle. In addition to work and school, Brooke is the worship leader at Victory in the Blood Church or VBC in Dallas, Texas.

As she pulled out of the parking lot adjacent to her boutique, Brooke decided to let Bradley stay over Granny Mae's house so she could get some sleep. After a quick stop at a local deli Brooke drove home. As she entered the door her Maltese snowball and a pile of mail greeted her at the door. As she placed her bags on the counter she sorted through her mail. Just then she came across a letter from VBC for a mandatory meeting for the worship team and band concerning a men's conference in July. Being annoyed, Brooke let out a long sigh. She was so tired of ministering during men's conferences. She was always approached by someone who hadn't been to church since he was five asking if he could take her on a date. Otherwise some clown would tell her he didn't know LisaRaye could sing. After compromising herself with Ryan resulting in single parenthood, Brooke vowed to wait on the Lord to send her husband. Unlike many women, she wasn't willing to settle for anything less.

Joelle paced the floor at Johns Hopkins hospital lost in her thoughts. "How could she be so reckless?" she muttered. A few months ago Joelle was reunited with her youngest three siblings: sister Josette(25) and brothers Johan(24) and Joey(23). Through a series of events that most people would consider coincidence but for people of faith could only be recognized as the hand of God, Joelle took in all three of them. Johan and Joey had become adjusted to their new life as a family but Josette has fought Joelle at every turn. This was the third time in 90 days that Josette has run off and now she was being hospitalized after a beating from her boyfriend. Joelle knew this life all too well and had struggled to live on the straight and narrow. Now her past was on her doorstep tormenting her like a schoolyard bully. Josette was the youthful spitting image of Joelle. She possessed the same survival skills and mindset that bound Joelle for years and it broke her heart to see her baby sister walk in her dead footsteps. Just last month Joelle had found seven thousand dollars in Josette's laundry and when she approached her about it Josette taunted Joelle saying "Go head and keep it, I know your god doesn't pay much." Joelle's blood boiled at Josette's words. Living right was a daily choice for Joelle and Josette had hit a nerve. In the past few years Joelle had purchased a row home in Catonsville and kept a 9 to 5 job as a senior aesthetician. Josette had no idea what Joelle's God was truly capable of doing. The nurse had startled Joelle from her thoughts when she tapped her shoulder. Still unable to hear on one side from her own abuse, Joelle turned to hear the nurse's words. "We were able to stop the internal bleeding but she does have a broken jaw and three broken ribs. You can see her briefly." Joelle entered the room to see Josette with tubes everywhere. Her heart broke all over again. She stroked her sister's hair and sobbed. In a still small voice the Lord said "This is how I felt when you were in her place." Joelle was flooded with heartache and gratitude at the exact same time. She asked "Lord, what do you need me to do?" He replied "Allow me to use you to stop destruction from claiming the others." "What others?" she quizzed. "The others I have waiting on you…" said the Lord. "Yes." was Joelle's reply. The doctor entered the room and told Joelle that Josette needed to rest. She gathered her things and headed to her car. When she made it home it was almost midnight. Johan and Joey were waiting up for her so she told them what had happened and the three of them prayed together before going to bed.

The next morning Joelle listened to the messages on her voicemail. The last call was from Lady Nora and Joelle returned her call first. Cheerful and chipper was Lady Nora as she answered the call "Hello my dear, I've been waiting to hear from you." "Hi mom." Joelle replied dryly. "What's the matter? I have great news." Lady Nora sang. "Josette was beaten by her boyfriend with a fractured jaw and broken ribs." said Joelle with tears welling in her eyes. "Oh my. We will keep her lifted up in prayer like we always do." said Lady Nora. "It's just like God to give someone something at a time like this." thought Lady Nora. "Well baby, I'm calling you because Elisha and I know it's time for you to be released." "Released from what?" Joelle asked. "Obscurity." said Lady Nora. "You will minister on opening night of the women's conference in June." "Huh?" said Joelle. "My life is on fire right now." she added. "Yes baby it is. Seek the Lord for your message." Lady Nora hung up the phone.

Apple walked into her apartment and was greeted by her son Silk and newest baby girl Chiffon. Ian was in the kitchen cooking and peaked around the corner to see her kiss the children. "Where's mine?" asked Ian. When Apple entered the kitchen Ian's countenance dropped when he saw her sad face. "What's wrong love?" he asked. Apple told Ian that she had lied to him about volunteering for the past seven months and had been going to therapy. Ian told her he already knew because she was on his insurance. Apple was never good at telling believable stories and she felt embarrassed by his words. Apple looked in his eyes and told him she was molested by her brother when she was a child and her mother punished her for it. Ian knew Apple had major issues and was glad she felt safe enough to open up. He assured her that he would continue to support her and love her as she was. Apple was finally married like she always wanted to be yet discovered it didn't cure her pain and insecurity. She and Ian got married two years ago a week before Chiffon was born. She had asked Ryan to marry them but he required the couples he marries to be a member in good standing of a local church for at least a year. Apple was heated and wasn't about to join a church in order to get married. She hasn't talked to Ryan or Blake since. As far as Apple was concerned they didn't want her to be happy and hid behind church protocol as their excuse. She and Ian found a minister to marry them at Druid Hill Park without any conditions at all. They met him, paid him and a week later he married them. It was just the two of them, the minister, Cashmere and Silk.

It was loud as usual in the Evans home during family dinner. It was Rhoda and Evans turn to host the weekly affair. Alex, Gavin, Josh, Beryl, Brice and Ryan were playing pool. Vivian, Alexis, Karen, Lisa, Victoria and Blake were watching an award show. Rhoda was setting the table while Evans took the food off of the grill and Beryl and Brice's sons were playing in the backyard.

During dinner Ryan announced his preaching engagement during July in Dallas. Since it was a Men's conference Evans and Gavin volunteered to travel with him and Ryan gladly accepted. They always acted like they were going as his armor bearers but usually told him to carry his own junk. They always get a kick out of pastors with huge entourages and would often crack jokes. They would chuckle for hours while Ryan shook his head. Ryan always threatened not to take the two of them anywhere but he loved his dads having his back. Blake felt good knowing their dads were going with him. It was a great safety net to have their family's support. Like Pastor Elisha always told them, God doesn't call a person he calls a family.

It was early June in Hampton, Virginia and yet again love was in the air. The families congregated in joy to witness the wedding ceremony of Alexis and Paris. The

Lovehall estate was buzzing with chefs, workman, and relatives. The wedding was set to take place during sunset in the botanical garden and the reception would be by candlelight under silk tents. The bridal tea was a huge success the week prior and now the big day had arrived. Grandpa Rhodes was in town cracking jokes with Evans, Parrish, and Gavin about Alex's father Charlie's sharkskin suit. Vivian knew her father always made fun of her father-in-law but pretended not to notice. Alex's mother Anita was also mortified by her husband's suit but after fifty two years of marriage chose her battles wisely. After all this was her granddaughter's day and Charlie was not going to ruin it. Vivian adored her mother in law. It was nice having a mother's love since her and Rhoda's mom passed away. Rhodes was a great father to them their whole lives and really went out of his way to make his girls feel loved. Parrish and Patricia were so tickled to have all three of their children married by the end of summer. They were most pleased with Paris since he went through a phase that kept them on their knees in prayer. They knew females were quite smitten with him and had prayed a host of thirsty, compromising, gold diggers away. They appreciated the way their youngest two children ran in the same circle which intertwined their families together. They were also pleased with the marriage Quinn and Texan had built together. Ryan stood at the outdoor altar with Paris and Coby as the processional began. Six bridesmaids including Nia and Quinn were escorted by six groomsmen including Texan,

Josh and Devin. The Emerald green and teal printed dresses were set off by peacock feathers in each bouquet. The dewy makeup of each bridesmaid brought a tropical feel to the evening. Logan was a junior bridesmaid and was escorted by one of Paris's nephews. As the band played and the singer sang, Ryan beamed as Blake walked down the aisle. He remembered their wedding day and how happy he was to have her as his wife. Her skin glowed and was accentuated by the solid emerald green dress she wore. After the flower girl and ring bearer refused to walk together Ryan announced for the crowd to stand in order to receive the bride. Lexi looked gorgeous as she walked down the aisle with Alex in her trumpet style gown with emerald green sash. Her makeup was flawless. She wore an updo entwined with a crystal head piece without a veil. She carried fresh calla lilies wrapped in emerald green silk and possessed the glow that only God himself can anoint a bride with. After an emotional vow exchange because Paris couldn't stop crying, they were officially Mr. and Mrs. Paris Lovehall. That evening the family dined on lobster and steak and danced all night long. The following morning the Lovehalls left for their ten day honeymoon in the Maldives. Parrish and Patricia gave each other a high five because they day went off without a hitch. They could now focus on their baby girl Nia who to their surprise didn't break the bank!

Joelle rocked back in forth in her chair in Lady Nora's suite at the church. She knew what God had called her to do but her nerves were on ten. It was the opening night of the annual women's conference that Lady Nora hosted. This year's theme was Beauty for Ashes in homage to the victories Lady Nora has seen come out of her accountability group with the same name. Joelle being one of the most powerful testimonies for God's glory would set the tone for the rest of the weekend. The conference runs from Wednesday to Saturday each year. Blake was sitting on the front row in anticipation for what Joelle was going to preach. Even thought they had grown apart Blake was happy to see Joelle on top. Rhoda, Vivian and Victoria were also in attendance. Praise and worship was awesome. The anointing laid heavily in the sanctuary as Joelle mounted the platform.

Joelle's nerves had disappeared once the anointing came upon her. The weight of it surprised her as well as her heightened awareness and wholeness. She gave honor to Pastor Elisha and Lady Nora and recognized a few distinguished guests including First Lady Blake Hairston. After a long pause she began to tell her story..."When Lady Nora first called me to be here tonight I was overwhelmed. I had just returned from my baby sister's hospital bed who had suffered a severe beating at the hand of her boyfriend and I was bombarded with the reminder of who I use to be." "I am the eldest of five who was raising my brothers and sisters because my parents were crack addicts. I was learning to survive in the streets of Baltimore before the age of ten and a childhood was something I never had. I know all about ashes." Joelle said fervently. "After my parents death we were separated and

14

one of my sisters died. I had found out that my deceased sister Carmen who was the second oldest was the only child of my parents who didn't belong to my father. She was the product of my father prostituting my mother for their drug money and my father made my mother name her Carmen to taunt my mother for being common." Said Joelle in full honesty. "My father had the audacity to ridicule her for being pregnant by someone he made her become intimate with. As the story was told to me, he wanted a big family so that we could work to support their habit." "When I was fifteen I was rescued at a Laundromat by my first boyfriend William who was twenty five and took me in. He gave me everything. He had a condo, a nice car and treated me like a princess. I would go to school with new clothes and a pocket full of money." "Once I began to become intimate with Will I gained an appetite for male attention. While he was taking care of us I began to cut school to have sex with other guys. I know all about ashes." Joelle felt the spirit of shame dislodge from her mind and became empowered by the Spirit of Truth. "William worked nights as a troubleshooter for a computer company and I began to invite men into our home and into our bed. It wasn't long before I got caught and William still forgave me." "He told me that I didn't think I was capable of being loved so I practice self-sabotage. He even paid for me to go to counseling but it wasn't long before I went back to my wild ways." "For five years he put up with my behavior including having to have two abortions before he let me go. I know all about ashes." Joelle's sermon began to build momentum and anticipation. For the next forty minutes Joelle shared her brokenness with the congregation and there wasn't a dry eye in the house. She spoke of giving herself away until she had nothing left.

"Then one day God turned on the lights and I saw what I had become; a woman for sale. God reached into the filth of what had become my life and changed me forever." "Now I stand here as a blood washed child of the most-high God redeemed and delivered from a sordid past." Said Joelle in a voice of triumph! "Over two thousand years ago a man named Jesus bore my filth and wickedness on the cross and went to hell in my place. But because he was without sin the grave couldn't hold him so he rose from the dead with all power in his hands and when he rose, I rose." "Somebody in here tonight needs to get up from some things." "Tell that trifling, abusive, no good male I'm not for sale! Joelle exclaimed. "I'm sold out to Jesus Christ. I'm not your door mat, your toilet seat or your toy, I'm not for sale!" The sanctuary roared in a spirit of victory as women began to see their own worth in Christ and began to yell "I'm not for sale!" Rhoda was so happy to see that Joelle was finally free. The once broken bird had found her wings. Blake cried tears of joy to see all that God had done in Joelle's life. Lady Nora was filled with gratitude because Joelle had finally made it through. Women flooded the altar during the altar call and were changed forever. All manner of healings and deliverance had taken place. Pastor Elisha had been watching from the back of the sanctuary and knew an Evangelist had just been born.

Joelle was on high after service and it took hours for her to come down. As the anointing left her body exhaustion took its place. Once she made it home she took a hot shower and got into the bed. Josette had been missing for two days but Joelle finally had the peace to put her in God's hands and quickly she fell asleep.The word had spread about "I'm Not for Sale" and the sermon sold like hot cakes. In four weeks over eight hundred units were sold, most of which were the DVD opposed to the CD. As God would have it copies of the DVD had made their way to Sloan and Apple. Sloan had received hers from a client and Apple received hers from Dr. Washington. Joelle was asked to minister all over town but the "I'm Not for Sale" message was exclusive to the women's conference. Some churches backed out as if it was disappointing that God gave her new sermons and other churches accepted that "I'm Not for Sale" couldn't be duplicated.

Brooke had a seven inch pile of mail on her table when she decided to go through it. She had been so busy with stiletto parties since receiving her summer inventory that she was behind in her chores. At one party two women came to blows over the last size 7 pair of Sophia Webster beaded sandals when the hostess kicked them both out and bought the shoes herself. As she shuffled through her mail she came across a manila envelope from VBC. She had been waiting for the itinerary for the men's conference so that she could tell Granny Mae when she would need help with Bradley. Just as she took a sip from her coconut water Brooke almost choked when she saw the event poster. "Pastor Ryan Hairston of Laurel, Maryland!" She couldn't believe her eyes. She immediately called Granny Mae to tell her. In response Granny Mae told Brooke that everything done in secret always comes to light. She told her to tell him the truth because the fullness of time had come. Still in shock and knowing Gran was right, Brooke went to his church website and saw the infamous Blake. Brooke began to cry because they looked so happy. Envy began to settle in when the Holy Ghost reminded Brooke that Blake didn't know just as Ryan didn't and at the end of the day they were both God's daughters. Repenting for her thoughts Brooke knew one thing, she didn't know what to expect but she was going to look cute.

Blake was helping Ryan pack for his trip to Dallas in the morning. She had sleepover plans with Rhoda and Victoria while the men were gone. It was Tuesday night and the conference was from Wednesday night through Saturday afternoon. Ryan was the speaker for Thursday evening. Ryan couldn't help but think about what Tevin had prophesied to him months earlier and wondered what was on the horizon. Tevin's prophecies had a way of manifesting in 90 days or less and he was a week shy of 90 days. He didn't want Blake to be concerned so he never shared the word with her. Ryan was just hours away from the shock of his life. The next morning the men flew into Dallas/Fort Worth without a hitch. Tevin had put them up in a room at the Dallas Omni Park West hotel. As they were settling in Tevin came to the room to say hello. The men shared laughs and jokes with one of them being that Ryan had to sleep on a cot because Gavin and Evans claimed the beds. Ryan knew his dads were jokesters and had every intention to make this a mini vacation for themselves. Tevin told Ryan all the speakers were meeting for lunch and invited everyone to come. Gavin and Evans said they had plans which gave Ryan the freedom to not have to look after them. At lunch the men became acquainted with each other. As usual there was a leader present who had to spew out his accomplishments putting a bad taste in everyone's mouth. Tevin made a mental note to never invite him to minister again. He worked really hard to keep his hands clean in ministry and valued integrity in the pulpit. The rest of the men knew Tevin well enough to know this was the last time they'd see this gentleman and let him brag on himself. After a while the man knew he hadn't impressed anyone and that nobody was playing his game. Ryan was just thankful his dads didn't come because they would've had a field day with him. The speakers separated for the afternoon with plans to meet in the lobby at 5pm for the 7pm meeting. Ryan went back to Tevin's room to catch up. Ryan told Tevin that he'd been thinking about what he said since he said it. Tevin told him he believes he'll know what he's dealing with by the end of the conference.

Granny Mae told Brooke to be prepared for the worse because men don't like surprises. Brooke sighed as she thought about the proper way to approach Ryan. She knew there would be a reception area for the speakers before and after the nightly festivities. She also knew the speakers would arrive by 5:45pm and that she had to lead worship at 7pm. Though she had to be color coordinated with the worship team in yellow and white Brooke still looked cute as planned. She wore a yellow ruffled blouse and white pencil skirt with yellow floral sling back peep toe pumps. Her hair was in a high bun and her face was beat. She wore feminine diamond jewelry and her favorite Bond no 9 perfume.

Brooke arrived at VBC with her stomach in knots. There was no turning back. She pretended to help the hospitality ministry when the director announced that the speakers had arrived. Brooke turned her back to the door so that she could gather her thoughts. The men entered the room and the hospitality workers began to introduce themselves in service to the speakers. Some of them made requests for things they wanted in the upcoming days but Ryan told the women they he would eat what they prepared. Hearing his voice made Brooke's knees weak and she wondered what tomorrow would be like. Just then one of the speakers said "Who is that young lady?" The director replied that's Brooke our worship leader who has come to give us an extra hand. "Brooke I want you to meet our guests," said the hospitality director. Brooke turned around to be introduced and she and Ryan's eyes met. Ryan couldn't believe his eyes. He remembered in that moment what he and Brooke shared and his heart began to race. Brooke was introduced to the speakers (one of whom was single and very interested) including Tevin and Ryan. When she reached out for Ryan's hand it was as if all the air was sucked out of the room. Brooke's mind was racing and she fought back tears. As the men made their plates Brooke uttered the words "Can we talk?" Ryan agreed and they walked out of the church's service entrance. Ryan couldn't believe he was standing across from the woman he once loved. Before Brooke could speak Ryan apologized. He told her he was wrong for breaking things off with her over the phone and refusing to give her the closure she needed. He told her he felt like a newborn when he became born again and no longer knew how to function in the world. He admitted to being over-zealous and cut off everything that would distract him from his new life including her. Their relationship was very physical and he knew he would fall if he was around her. She accepted his apology and explanation. She remembered the vulnerability she felt after being born again too. It's like learning to live all over again. She told Ryan she needed his apology as well. Ryan told her she didn't do anything wrong and it was all him. She said she did need his forgiveness and he asked why. "Because I never told you about our son." said Brooke. Just then Ryan's heart dropped to his feet and shock set into his stomach. We have a five year old son. I found out I was pregnant during winter break and wanted to tell you to your face so I waited for you to come back to school but you would never see me. Ryan knew Brooke was telling the truth and wondered why he had been so cruel to her. "I need to see him." Ryan replied. Brooke took a photo out of her skirt pocket and Ryan was floored. Looking back at him were his eyes, nose and mouth. "His name is Bradley Michael." Brooke said. Ryan placed the picture in his suit jacket pocket and pulled Brooke close to him. He held her for about a minute before Blake crossed his mind. He let Brooke go and said "Wait, I'm married. How am I gonna tell this to my wife?" Ryan was overcome by a sense of panic and began to pace in the parking lot. Brooke told him they should go back inside but Ryan couldn't breathe. He told her to go ahead and she did. When Brooke ran into Tevin he asked her where Ryan was and she told him he was outside. Tevin opened the door to see Ryan sitting on the curb rocking. Tevin went over to Ryan in concern. He told Tevin he needed to go back to the hotel. Tevin knew something major had transpired so he put Ryan in the car and told the driver to drive Ryan back to the hotel and gave the driver a $50 bill. When Ryan entered the hotel room Gavin and Evans were having a food fest. Gavin announced "Here comes the fun police. We were gonna come tomorrow to hear you preach. We're on vacation." After a hardy laugh Gavin realized his son was in agony. The two men put down their hot wings and asked Ryan what was wrong. Ryan broke down in tears and cried the ugly cry. An hour later Ryan had finally told them what transpired and the three of them sat in silence.

When they saw Bradley they knew he was Ryan's child but they also knew the news would rock his marriage to its core.

Brooke was relieved by Ryan's reaction. When he held her he felt like everything was going to be alright. She felt light as a feather after releasing her secret and that night she sang like never before.

Apple watched Joelle's DVD over and over again. She had no idea that people told that kind of truth in church. She thought church was for perfect people who had no problems. She spent so much time being jealous of Joelle when she and Blake were best friends that she had no idea they had things in common. She knew abuse and promiscuity too. Apple decided to go hear Joelle speak at Dr. Washington's church the following week. Maybe there is something to this Jesus stuff after all.

Rhoda, Victoria and Blake were having a girl's weekend. Each night they'd sleep at a different house to watch movies and eat fab foods. Tonight they were watching only Denzel Washington movies and eating crab cakes and fried shrimp. Thursday was Christian Bale films with steak and lobster and Friday was Angelina Jolie films with grilled salmon and clams casino. They were so into their own plans that they didn't notice that the men hadn't called.

After service Tevin came to Ryan's room. Ryan told Tevin what had transpired and for the first time Tevin wished his prophesy had been wrong. The men decided to agree in prayer that God would get the glory through his trial. That night Ryan couldn't sleep. Gavin and Evans told him that telling Blake should be done face to face so he had to look alive until they got home. Ryan knew he had to see Bradley before he left town. He also knew he was going to take care of his son and make it work. Not only did he have to face Blake but together they had to stand before the congregation.

The next morning the men called the women together. They each had the phone on speaker and the men kept it together for the family's sake. At breakfast Tevin told Ryan that one of the ministers grilled a hospitality worker about Brooke and found out she owned a shoe store. Tevin had the address and told Ryan to go see about his son and he would distract the other minister from going. Ryan arrived to Brooke's boutique in a taxi. When he walked in she was pleasantly surprised. Brooke had been pulling shoes for a stiletto party on Saturday night. "Do you forgive me?" Brooke inquired. "I do" Ryan replied. "Can I see him?" "Of course you can." Brooke beamed. Just then a flower delivery arrived from the minister who admired her. Ryan was a bit jealous even though he wasn't with Brooke. He had to admit she was a knockout. Brooke closed the store and drove Ryan to Granny Mae's house to meet Bradley. Ryan was impressed with how well Brooke provided for their son. She told him she was getting her masters and that Bradley was in private school. Ryan told her he would start sending her money though Brooke wasn't looking for finances she was looking for him to be a father. When they arrived at Granny Mae's house Ryan began to feel weak. Brooke introduced Ryan to Granny Mae. Gran thought Ryan was handsome and said "I would've had your baby too." Ryan smiled and Brooke was mortified. Bradley was in the backyard on the swings. Brooke called him into the house and he lit up when he saw her. When he walked in the living room Ryan fought back tears. "Do you know who this is?" Brooke asked Bradley. He shook his head "Yes." "Who is he?" Brooke asked. "He's my daddy" said Bradley in a soft voice. Ryan's heart melted when his mini him knew who he was. "How did you know it was me?" Ryan quizzed. "Because we have the same face." Bradley replied. Granny Mae wiped the tears from her face and left the room so the three of them could bond. That evening Ryan mounted the platform a broken man. Ironically his sermon was about being a man of integrity. Ryan quoted his text and prayed. Even under the anointing his heart was heavy. He went to a new level in God as he ministered to the men. He was preaching the greatest sermon of his life. The power of God moved mightily but he was in pain. He had reached that difficult place where he could help others heal but was shattered himself. Ryan finally understood the term "leading while bleeding." On Friday Ryan kept Brooke's car to spend the day with Bradley. He had spoken to Blake that morning and felt even worse than he did before. He knew she would have a hard time adjusting to him having another priority. The truth was that Bradley was his son before Blake was his wife and even though she was unaware he existed they were now a package deal.

Ryan decided not to go to service in order to spend his evening with Bradley. When it was time to leave he told his son he would see him soon and that he loved him. Leaving an innocent five year old was the hardest thing Ryan had ever done. Departing Dallas was like leaving a piece of himself behind. When the men landed at BWI airport, Rhoda was there to pick them up. Blake was with Nia doing wedding stuff and Victoria was spending the day with Josh. When Evans and Rhoda got home he filled her in on what happened. Rhoda's heart was broken for her only child. She knew Blake would take it hard. Gavin told Victoria what happened when she got home and her heart was broken. When she saw the picture of her grandchild she couldn't believe her eyes. Ryan sat on the couch for over four hours for Blake to get home. She was on the phone when she walked in to greet him but knew by the look on his face it was time to hang up. "We need to talk." escaped Ryan's mouth and Blake was immediately afraid. Women use that phrase far too often but if a man says it, it's crucial. "Remember when I told you about the girl I was seeing in undergrad who I broke up with when we were getting back together?" asked Ryan "Yes." Blake replied. "I never told you but I broke up with her over the phone and refused to see her when she asked to meet up." Ryan said. "Okay." Blake replied. "She left school a few weeks later and I never saw or spoke to her again." Ryan explained. "What's the point?" Blake asked. Ryan felt himself being annoyed by her tone and replied "The point *is* she lives in Dallas, goes to the church I preached at and I found out that she and I have a five year old son." The attitude Blake gave Ryan was crushed by his words. Pain welled inside of her and she regretted her condescending tone. "You have a son?" "Yup." Ryan replied. Blake began to think about her image and how Ryan having a son made her look. Her hurt turned into anger and she was offended. "How dare he come home with a five year old son behind her back?" Blake thought. He was going to pay dearly for her embarrassment. Knowing full well that Blake was thinking all the wrong things, Ryan went to his man cave to call Josh. Blake called Rhoda to tell her what happened and she said she already knew because daddy told her. Blake told Rhoda that she wasn't about to be with a man who brings kids home like Kenneth. Rhoda reminded Blake that Ryan had a son before she was his wife and that Ryan is nothing like her father. She told Rhoda she would look like a fool in front of everyone and Ryan and his child could have a great life without her. Rhoda was disappointed by Blake's attitude. Never once did she consider Ryan's dilemma of having a child in the world he knew nothing about. "That girl is probably a hot mess anyway." Blake said. Rhoda was through with Blake's attitude. "Now you wait a minute Miss First Lady you're not acting like the child I raised nor the wife Ryan married. You sit and tell women how to stand by their husbands and submit to God's design for marriage now it's your turn to walk the walk. Asking Ryan to deny an innocent child is asking Ryan not to be a man. You better take your place beside him and lead by example. Baby girl it's time to love like you've never loved before. What if daddy had that attitude toward you? He accepted you because he loves me and it's time for you to grow up. Now I know you're hurt but for one second can you think about your husband's needs over your appearance? You're starting to act like Joelle back when she was putting on airs. While you're alone with God you need to figure out when you got on that high horse because if you don't get off it I will knock you off of it myself. Goodnight!" Rhoda said as she hung up the phone. Rhoda's words stung Blake like a hive full of bees. She knew Ryan's son was innocent but she's worked hard to maintain their image.

Josh was always a comfort to Ryan. He always made Ryan feel better. Josh agreed to be in his nephew's life and help out any way he could. Victoria realized that Ryan was on the phone and asked Josh to pass the receiver. "Hi honey how are you feeling?" she quizzed "I'll be alright." Ryan replied. "Daddy showed me Bradley's picture he is a beautiful child. Just know dad and I have your back no matter what." Victoria responded. "Thanks mom." Ryan said dryly wishing her words were Blake's words. After hanging up Ryan decided to call Bradley before taking a shower and sleeping in the basement.

Rhoda told Evans what happened with Blake. She couldn't believe she would compare Ryan to Kenneth. Evans knew he had to talk to his baby girl and together they prayed for Blake and Ryan's marriage to weather the storm.The following morning word had spread throughout the family concerning Ryan's discovery of Bradley. Everyone shared the same sentiment that Ryan and Blake needed the family's support more than ever. When Nia reached out to Blake in support for her and Ryan, Blake felt betrayed by her bestie and stopped answering her calls. "How could everyone think its okay that Ryan had a child behind my back?" Blake thought. Blake was unable to see that Ryan was just as surprised, hurt and shocked as she was but offense had set in and Blake was walking in deception. Nobody was trying to trivialize her pain but everyone knew God was able to keep them in their season of trial.

Over the next few weeks Blake allowed the atmosphere in her home to become cold and distant. She had stopped praying and refused to speak to Ryan or go to church. After 2 Sundays had passed the family decided to stand by Ryan as he told the congregation of GLC what the family is dealing with.

On Sunday morning the Hairstons and Evans stood before the congregation of GLC as Ryan told the flock about Bradley. Rhoda then asked if she could speak and Ryan passed her the mic. Evans had a smirk on his face because he knew his wife was a sass muffin from way back. "I just want to say that our son and daughter have labored for you all before the Lord since this church was founded. They've fasted and prayed for you, paid some of your bills and sacrificed their time and efforts for the benefit of the flock. If you are unable to lift them up in prayer and support them in their season of trial, you need not to return next week. If you want to make this into a scandal instead of a time to love, we ask that you remove yourself from their covering. For all of you who are indeed Ryan's sheep we thank you for loving our family as we have loved yours." said Rhoda with a "don't mess with my children" tone.

95% of the congregation stood in support of their under shepherd as a couple handfuls of folks walked out. Once it was obvious who was staying and who was leaving service began as usual.

Chapter 2: Forgiveness

Joelle mounted the platform of Let the Redeemed of the Lord say so church to a packed house. She ministered from the theme "Kiss Your Past Goodbye". She shared a few personal stories that once again left no dry eyes in the house. Women could be heard crying out as a witness to their own struggles. One woman in particular, Apple, was amazed yet again by her transparency. She began to feel a hot sensation encompass her body and a sense of urgency crept into her spirit. Joelle opened the altar to a somber and broken audience. This wasn't the "I'm Not for Sale" crowd this was the "Lord if you don't step in I will not make it." crowd. Apple arose from her seat completely on fire and walked to the front of the sanctuary. Joelle was surprised to see her and stepped off the platform to lay hands on her. Apple felt the power of God separate her from the shame and hurt she has lived with since she was nine years old. Joelle led the group in the prayers of salvation and restoration. As she walked to the opposite side of the platform to give a woman a word of knowledge she recognized Sloan standing in the crowd weeping. After giving the woman a word Joelle was moved with God's love and wrapped her arms around Sloan who kept crying "Please forgive me, I'm sorry." Joelle told Sloan that she forgave her a long time ago. Just then Joelle's ear opened and her hearing was fully restored. Little did she know, she was about to cross paths with another person from her past.

Dr. Washington had made her way to Apple and rocked her in her arms. As God would have it Dr. Washington was not just a therapist she was also an ordained minister. She told Apple that she'd walk with her through the process and for the first time in decades Apple was at peace. Joelle left the platform in a weeping praise and the service was brought to a close.

Blake hadn't spoken to Ryan in weeks and they were just days away from Nia and Devin's wedding. Nia couldn't believe how Blake was acting and found her behavior quite hypocritical since Blake was always handing out advice. Nia's sister Quinn was on standby just in case Blake flaked on her. The wedding would take place on a private yacht on the Patomac River at sunset. Blake and Ryan would be the only people in the wedding party and the reception would be held on the top deck for an intimate crowd of fifty guests. Nia decided to call Rhoda to express her concerns. Rhoda was furious with Blake. Nia had planned Blake's wedding and was there for her the entire step of the way. Rhoda was two seconds from rocking Blake's world. She told Nia to give her an hour and she would call her back. Rhoda hung up the phone and called Blake. "Hello." said Blake. "Hello my behind, are you standing up for Nia this Friday or not?" Rhoda quizzed. "I don't feel like being around anyone right now." Blake said dryly. "How convenient you selfish piece of work, you're really starting to tick me off." Rhoda chided. "So you're not going to support your best friend on the most important day of her life because of your own selfishness?" "It's not that." Blake whined. "It's exactly that! I guess if you can't love and support your own husband the rest of us don't stand a chance" Rhoda mocked. "Mom don't say that." Blake said as she began to cry. "It's the truth are you going or not?" said Rhoda "Yes I'm going." Blake answered. "Well let me tell you one thing. This is Nia and Devin's day, do not make it about you or your feelings or you and I will have a major problem. Call Nia and apologize for your selfishness and tell her you'll be there for her." Rhoda instructed. "I will." Blake responded.

Blake immediately called Nia because she knew that Rhoda was "not the one." She apologized, Nia accepted and the two of them made up. She decided she would go to the wedding but she still wasn't speaking to Ryan.

It was late Friday afternoon when the guests boarded the private yacht on the National Harbor to celebrate Nia and Devin. Devin's family had flown in from Chicago the previous night and love was in the air. The guests mingled and noshed on clam cakes and chowder flown in from Horton's in Rhode Island. Over their years of traveling as a family, the Lovehalls loved the food in New England. The reception meal was a Clam Bake. Parrish and Patricia were still taken back by the easy breezy wedding Nia wanted. They had spent so much money on

Quinn's wedding that they were queasy when Nia got engaged.

At sunset Ryan and Devin stood with the officiant as Blake walked to the altar. She wore a floor length pastel yellow dress and carried one long stemmed calla lily. The guests stood as Nia walked out escorted by Parrish in a floor length white dress. Her makeup was minimal and her hair was in a messy bun but she had the glow. The vows were exchanged and the minister introduced Mr. and Mrs. Devinshire Braxton. Ryan snickered because he forgot that Devin was Devinshire. Gavin and Evans looked at each and shook their heads as they laughed too.

During the reception everyone began calling Devin, Devinshire and asking him for Grey Poupon, to play cricket or meet them in the study. Everyone laughed and had a great time and nobody noticed that Blake refused to talk to Ryan. The following morning the Braxtons left for their honeymoon in Greece.

The following Friday during family dinner Ryan announced that he was sending for Bradley and Brooke. He wanted to give Bradley a 6th birthday party and introduce him to the family. Everyone agreed to help but Blake went off! "How dare you flaunt your love child and baby's momma in my face! I hate you so much for ruining my life and I hate all of you for helping him!" Rhoda stood up from the table to slap Blake in the mouth but Evans pulled her back. Ryan looked at Blake with tears in his eyes and told her he was sorry that she hated him but he wasn't going to deny his own child. "Then you need to be with Brooke and Bradley and divorce me" Blake snapped.

Later that evening Ryan called Rhoda because Blake didn't come home. Rhoda told him she wasn't at her house and would call around to look for her. The next morning Rhoda found out from Lexi that Blake was staying with Vivian and Alex. Rhoda was hot as fish grease and called her sister. Evans sat on the edge of the bed to listen. "Good morning." Vivian sang into the phone. "Please tell me that Blake isn't at your house." Rhoda threatened. "She *is* my niece Rhoda and she needs to stay here for a while." Vivian responded. "Vi, she's a married woman and has no business moving out of her husband's home, she isn't battered! She has to learn to stick it out and be an adult, chided Rhoda. "She wants some time to herself to figure things out." said Vivian. "Vi, you don't let married people who aren't abused move into your house, you let them fix their marriages on their own." exclaimed Rhoda. "I'm not putting my niece out Rhoda." Vivian snapped. "I'll tell you what, you got one hour to put her out of your house or I'm coming over to burn it down." said Rhoda as she hung up the phone. Evans was cracking up. "Girl I knew you were gangster. Is she serious? Blake had no reason to leave that house. I spoke to her a couple weeks ago and she told me she would try to work it out", Evans added. "This situation would be completely different if the child was under 3,

Evans. He is two years older than their marriage."
explained Rhoda. "I hear you sweet Rhoda, all we can do
is what we've been doing." said Evans.

A half an hour later Blake called Rhoda from home
and said Vivian asked her to leave because Rhoda was
crazy. Rhoda told Blake to never leave her home if she
isn't a battered woman. Blake told Rhoda she felt
threatened by Brooke and felt like she had an advantage
for having Ryan's first child. Rhoda told her that was a
conversation she needed to have with Ryan.

Blake went into Ryan's man cave to finally begin a
dialogue. He was surprised as she sat beside him and laid
her head on his shoulder. "I'm jealous of her." Blake
blurted out. "You have no reason to be. You're my wife
and I chose you." Ryan said sincerely. "Is she pretty?"
asked Blake. "She is." said Ryan. "I don't want you to
leave me." Blake said crying. "I don't want you to leave
me either." Ryan replied. That afternoon Blake and Ryan
talked like two married adults about their friendship,
marriage and expectations for the future. They made
agreements and laid out a plan to move forward as a unit.
Blake expressed her feelings of hurt over what Kenneth
had done and admitted she compared Ryan to her father.
They agreed she would seek help from a therapist twice
per week for as long as it took.Blake called Rhoda to make
amends. Her mother then gave her the sympathy and
attention she was seeking since she handled the matter
with maturity. Blake was learning how to love Ryan

despite her pain and Ryan was learning to trust Blake with his.

Brooke was nervous as she and Bradley walked through the doors of BWI airport. Ryan and Blake were pulling out of the cell phone lot and on their way to pick them up. The police barely gave travelers the opportunity to be dropped off and picked up without rushing folks along. Brooke wore a maxi dress, Giuseppe Zanotti firewings sandals, Jimmy Choo Beatrix sunglasses and a high ponytail. Her makeup was dewy and she looked like a million bucks.

Blake was nervous as she and Ryan pulled out of the cell phone lot. She made Nia choose her outfit through face time to make sure she looked her best. Blake wore a maxi dress, some jeweled flat sandals, oversized shades, a high bun and dewy makeup. She too looked like a million bucks.

As Ryan pulled his truck to the curb Bradley began to jump up and down. Blake couldn't believe how much he looked like Ryan. Ryan opened her door to let her out of the car and immediately introduced Brooke to Blake. Though they were both sizing each other up with knots in their stomachs, they embraced in a hug. Ryan picked Bradley up and began to swing him around as he laughed. He told Bradley that Blake was his wife and his stepmom and he hoped they could be friends. Bradley said okay and told Blake it was nice to meet her.

For the week long duration of their stay, Brooke would be staying at Gavin and Victoria's house and Bradley would stay where ever he was comfortable. Bradley's birthday party would take place the following afternoon in place of family dinner at Ryan and Blake's home. On the way to Gavin and Victoria's house the adults made small talk while Bradley played with Brooke's IPad. Ryan was relieved that the initial introduction had taken place but he knew women were just as territorial as men. He had the tough job of making sure that Blake felt secure and Brooke felt respected. No wife wants to be reminded of the love her husband once shared with someone else and no woman wants to be disregarded because her child's father has a wife. He had to admit his work was cut out for him but it was important for him to have Blake's support.

Upon arrival at the Hairston home Victoria and Gavin stood in the door anxiously waiting to see Bradley. They had already met Brooke during visits to Wilberforce. When the Hairstons saw Bradley it was like seeing Ryan at six all over again. "Hi baby, I'm your Ganny." Victoria shouted. Just then Bradley ran up to her and wrapped his arms around her neck. She couldn't fight back the tears and wouldn't let him go. Gavin got choked up when he saw Bradley as well but managed not to cry. Everyone went inside the house where Gavin had already picked up some takeout from a local soul food spot.

That evening the Hairstons talked and fellowshipped over barbecued ribs, fried fish, cole slaw, macaroni and cheese, sweet potato cake and brown sugar lemonade. Ryan asked Brooke if he could change Bradley's last name to Hairston which he and Blake had already discussed and she agreed. Victoria could sense Blake's sadness and called her into the laundry room. While there she expressed to Blake how appreciative she was for not making her son choose and that having Bradley did not negate the fact that Ryan loved her. Blake told Victoria she was standing by her husband and knew that her pain would heal in time.

Once back in the dining room Victoria told Brooke she would take her to her room so she could unpack. Victoria told Brooke she was just as welcomed in her and Gavin's home as Bradley. She went on to say that because Brooke had their first grandchild she would always be special and though they didn't know her well, she was still family. Brooke thanked her for her sentiments and also added that she respected the fact that Ryan was married and her only motivation was to allow her son to know his father.

After a few hours of family time and laughing at Josh's reaction to Bradley, Ryan and Blake were heading home. Bradley wanted to stay with his mother so Ryan didn't press the issue and he told Bradley he should get good rest because his birthday party was the next day.

On the way home Blake was relieved that the night was over and her anxiety had subsided. She told Ryan that Bradley was his spitting image and the cutest little boy ever. Ryan told Blake there were more cute babies where Bradley came from and she told him she wanted one too. Ryan was surprised because Blake wanted to wait five years for children. He then told her they could start trying as soon as she stopped all measures of preventing pregnancy and she told him she would.

As Joelle was preparing to meet Lady Nora for lunch she had received the call she'd been waiting for. It had been 21 days since she last saw Josette during her third disappearance of the summer. "Ms. Clarke, this is detective Perry Manning of the Baltimore County Police Department. We found your sister." "Okay", Joelle hesitantly said. "She has been living illegally in a public storage bin with her boyfriend." said detective Manning. Joelle was relieved because "found" could've meant the worse. Joelle called Lady Nora to cancel but she asked if she could go with her and the two women went to get Josette. During the ride Lady Nora offered and Joelle accepted to place Josette in a Christian program for troubled young women from ages 21-30 in Arizona. The program had a 98% success rate and it was worth a try to save Josette's young life.Joelle needed the peace as did her brothers. Joelle was wise enough to know that the enemy was using Josette to distract, disrupt and destroy what God was trying to do in her life. After preaching at Dr. Washington's church she was approached by William

Parks in the church parking lot. She couldn't believe how her life had come full circle and apologized to William when she saw him. He told her she was young and it wasn't her fault and he apologized for beginning an intimate relationship with her at such a young age. Tears came to his eyes as he told her he should've protected her instead. Over the next half hour Joelle learned that he was in ministry, had been married for six years and had three children. As if a ton of weight was removed from their shoulders they parted ways with full closure from their past indiscretions.

Apple was making great strides under the watchful eye of Dr. Washington. Ian had come for a few sessions and their marriage was growing. They started going to church as a family and the children's behavior had improved. Silk was no longer spitting on people and Chiffon stopped throwing tantrums. Dr. Washington told Apple it was now time to go deeper into the therapeutic process. It was time to include Mrs. Brown.

Blake shook violently as tears fell across her apricot cheeks and into her ears. After two weeks of therapy she decided to be honest with Dr. Agbadou. As she laid on the deep eggplant leather coach she finally told the truth. She was jealous of Brooke, was ticked off at Ryan, wished Bradley didn't exist and was hurt by her mother. Blake was tired of acting like she was okay with her new life. Every time she walked into the church she felt like a fool. She felt as if people either pitied her or were amused by her pain. She was mad at Rhoda for accepting Bradley and taking Ryan's side. She was jealous of Brooke because she had Ryan's first child. Blake even felt like she was no longer special since being raped because it meant Ryan wasn't the only man she'd been with. Dr. Agbadou had her work cut out for her. She knew the core of Blake's pain was her perception and hoped she'd have a breakthrough before living two lives got the best of her.

Joelle was enjoying a rare September breeze on the terrace of a local bakery, when he walked up and introduced himself. "Hello beautiful, my name is Josiah Carter." he said. "Nice to meet you. I'm Joelle Clarke." "Yes I know, I'm familiar with your ministry." Josiah replied. "How so?" Joelle inquired. "My aunt has been playing your DVD for weeks." answered Josiah. In the back of her mind Joelle was relieved that she didn't have to explain her life to another person. Josiah asked if he could call her and she said yes. He placed her number in his phone and offered her his. Joelle declined and told him she'd get his number when he called her. As he walked away she realized for the first time in her life she didn't size him up, calculate the price of his garments nor use her looks to seduce him, God was definitely real.

A week later Joelle found herself at Bob Evans on a breakfast fellowship with Josiah. She wore a pair of jeans, crisp white shirt, a plaid blazer and ballerina flats. Of course her makeup was flawless but she wore her glasses and a messy bun. No pretense, no hidden agenda, just

Joelle. Over a hot plate of the homestead breakfast Joelle learned that Josiah was raised in the house of the Lord and had an older brother who drowned in a swimming pool when he was four. Raised an only child in Charlotte, North Carolina Josiah's father was a retired Marine and his mother was a retired Nurse. Josiah moved to Maryland when his favorite aunt on his father's side Minnie, got him a job at the NSA. Josiah was a data analyst with a bachelor's degree from UNC Charlotte in Finance and a master's degree from Queens University in Executive Coaching. He had no children, was active in church and had been celibate for six years. Joelle couldn't believe her ears. A grown man who is saving himself for his wife, what a gem! Joelle shared that she was caring for her siblings, was an aesthetician by profession but wanted to open a crisis center for battered and abused women. The two of them talked for over three hours and agreed to see one another again.

Blake was still wearing a mask on the surprise anniversary cruise their parents planned for her and Ryan's third anniversary. She smiled in the pictures, played games and kept up her façade. On the inside she was a raging river. She imagined herself holding Rhoda down in the pool or beating Ryan with a bat. Evans noticed something was off with Blake. He had been on the planet too long and experienced too much to not recognize her demeanor. He planned to take her to dinner when they got back home to get to the bottom of things. His baby girl was off track and he refused to ignore it. In the middle of paradise all Blake could think about was her anger and pain.

Nia and Devin were settling into their new life in Chicago. Devin's case load was heavy as he sought to make partner and began to work twelve hour shifts at the firm. Nia didn't expect to spend so much time away from her husband so early in their marriage. She understood how her mom must've felt when Parrish spent so many hours at work. She had just worked her first day at an elementary school just minutes from their high rise and couldn't share her day with Devin so she dialed her mom in Hampton. After expressing her concerns her mom eased her mind. She told Nia that they were in the building stage of marriage and that it takes a while to get where older couples are. Patricia told Nia not to compare herself to her and her father or any other couple because every couple has their own path and process. Nia felt better when she hung up with her mother and heated up some leftovers from the night before.

Mrs. Brown refused to go to therapy with Apple. She mocked her for seeking therapy and accused Apple of acting like white folks. She told Apple she better not be in therapy shaming their family nor airing her dirty laundry. Apple in her new found strength told Mrs. Brown that she is finally able to admit what Chester did to her and that it wasn't her fault. Mrs. Brown told Apple that Chester did nothing to her. In a moment of hurt and dismissal Apple told Mrs. Brown if she had been a better mother she wouldn't have a child molester and rapist for a son. Just then Mrs. Brown punched Apple in the mouth knocking out her front tooth. Blood filled Apple's mouth as she stormed out the door. Mrs. Brown collapsed to her knees and cried as she realized their secret was made known.

Josiah and Joelle held hands as they left the matinee show at Sight and Sound. They were headed to have a late lunch in Amish country. They had been keeping each other company for over a month and were great friends. Josiah wanted to introduce Joelle to his parents and the two of them along with Aunt Minnie were driving to Charlotte the following week. Josiah knew Joelle would be his wife but he wanted to court her properly. After a private meeting with Pastor Elisha who was the closest person she had to a father, he made his intentions known. Pastor Elisha was honored that Josiah would come to him and offered him some biblical advice on how to proceed.

It had been a month since the school year began and Nia was in the back of her classroom helping a student when shots rang out. Before she could shut and lock her classroom door bullets were flying into her classroom. It wasn't until she and all the children were laying on the floor that she saw several of her students had been hit. When she called out to her students all responded except one. She crawled to retrieve her cell phone and dial 911. Gunfire could still be heard in the distance though Nia managed to shut and lock her classroom door. The 911 operator asked her where in the school she was located because they were already aware of the situation. She gave them an update on the hurting students and began CPR on the unresponsive child. Knowing she was new to school the assistant principal made his way to her classroom door. He made himself known so she would unlock it. He stepped in as Nia couldn't help the student regain his breath. They tried for over 15 minutes to resuscitate the child. Nia decided to do what she knew to do. She broke school policy, protocol and procedure and began to pray.

As the car pulled into the driveway of the Carter home in Charlotte, Joelle was excited to meet Josiah's parents. They had to be some awesome individuals to raise such an intelligent, thoughtful and kind son. She imagined them to be loving and warm since the apple doesn't fall far from the tree. Aunt Minnie was so sweet so she knew the Carter's had to be wonderful people. Josiah knocked on the door even though he had a key. He wanted his parents to meet them at the door. When the door opened Melvin Carter Sr. answered the door. After hugging his son he was introduced to Joelle. He was pleased that his son found a looker. He welcomed her with open arms and told her to come in. He teased his sister for being old and the two of them laughed. The four of them laughed in the den as they waited for Rose. Rose hadn't come home yet from volunteering at the shelter. She would give free medical help a few days per week. As they sat talking and drinking lemonade Rose entered the house through the back door. Joelle was anticipating her arrival seeing as though Mr. Carter was so endearing. Rose yelled for Josiah to get the bags out of her car. He immediately got up and helped his mother bring bags of groceries into the house. She made small talk with him in the kitchen knowing full well that Joelle and Minnie were in the den. Melvin yelled to Rose to come greet their guests. She said she'd be there in a minute. When Josiah returned to the den he sat back down next to Joelle. Almost ten minutes had transpired since Melvin told her to come. When Rose entered the den and saw Joelle her countenance fell. She ignored her and spoke to Minnie. Then she turned to Joelle and said hello in a dry, cold voice. Joelle still smiling said it was nice to finally meet her and Rose replied 'yes and you too." Joelle turned to Josiah and asked what was wrong and he said she was probably tired.

During dinner Rose grilled Joelle. She was so disappointed that her son would bring home someone from a broken home, who had no college degree and to add insult to injury she was light skinned. Josiah was raised to appreciate his beautiful black sisters and yet he showed up with her. This girl may have been beautiful by society's standards but she knew four beautiful brown girls who had far more to offer Josiah than Miss Joelle.

Nia's nerves were shot once she made it home. Thank God the prayers of the righteous availed much because her student had pulled through. She had left 16 messages on Devin's cell, had his parents call him and still he couldn't be reached. Parrish and Patricia had just landed and were on their way to Devin and Nia's condo. When the Lovehalls arrived they were so grateful their daughter was safe. Parrish told Patricia if Devin couldn't do his job, Nia had to come home. The Lovehalls set up in the spare bedroom and Patricia ordered delivery for them to eat. The shooting had occurred ten minutes after ten o'clock that morning and it was now five thirty and Devin hadn't responded to Nia's calls. At six thirty Devin finally called stating that he had been in a closed deposition all day and that nobody knew about the shooting. When he arrived home Parrish was waiting for him. Just like he told Pat he told Devin, "If you can't handle your job as her husband, my daughter is coming home." Devin despised being scolded in his own home but knew not to play with Parrish. He apologized and told him he'd do better. Parrish told him it might be a good idea to take care of his wife instead of chasing a dollar. Devin became offended. Parrish didn't care. Devin was not about to give up his paycheck to be at home by five, Nia would adjust like every other attorney's wife.

Blake sat across from Evans at dinner thinking she had everyone fooled. "You gonna tell me the truth baby girl?" asked Evans. "About what Dad?" Blake responded. About the fake disposition you've been walking around with. Blake sat in silence knowing she couldn't lie to Evans. "I'm hurt." she responded. "I know." said Evans. "The thing I don't understand is why are you acting like you're not hurt." Blake told him because everyone expects her not to be. Evans told her that nobody expects her to act like things are easy. As a family they are just asking her to walk in love. Blake told him everything she shared with Dr. Agbadou. Evans's heart broke for his daughter like it did when he heard about her assault. He told her he would keep this situation between them two but that she had to get to the root of her pain. Blake confided in him that Dr. Agbadou wanted her to forgive and release Kenneth. Evans's eye twitched as he thought about the run in they had but knew it was necessary for his baby girl to heal. He agreed to drive her to Connecticut to get closure from her biological dead beat of a father.

Rose Carter called Josiah to tell him he was moving too fast with Joelle. How could he know she was his wife over the course of a month? It took Melvin six years to marry her. Rose told Josiah she was sure Joelle was a nice young lady but he needed someone who brought more to the table. Josiah told his mother he was marrying Joelle the following year and that she was an awesome woman and being from a broken home and not having an opportunity to pursue an education did not make Joelle unsuitable for him. He reminded her that the same God she claims to serve is the same God who will redeem the life the enemy stole from Joelle. Rose felt ashamed, her son had never corrected her before. Deep down Rose was afraid of losing him to Joelle. Since Melvin Jr. died Josiah became her world. Her marriage to Melvin Sr. wasn't the best and she thought someone like Joelle didn't deserve a man like her son. Rose told Josiah she would try to accept Joelle but Josiah told her their relationship would not be based on her acceptance. Rose hung up the phone and threw herself a pity party.

It was a crisp fall day when Evans pulled his Yukon up to the Elm Street Oyster House in Greenwich, Connecticut. Blake was scheduled to meet Kenneth for lunch and Evans had planned to wait in the truck while watching a DVD and eating the lunch he'd prepared that morning. Evans told Blake if Kenneth popped off he'd be in jail by the evening, to make her smile. With knots in her stomach, Blake entered the restaurant and saw Kenneth waiting at a table in the corner. Kenneth stood up to greet her and when he wrapped his arms around her Blake began to cry. Kenneth took the hankie out of his pocket and wiped her tears and for the first time saw the pain he left in her soul. He grew ashamed of himself knowing what his actions so many years ago had caused. As they sat at the table Kenneth waited for over ten minutes for Blake to form her words. Finally she blurted out, "I can't forgive my husband because I haven't forgiven you." Kenneth inquired why she needed to forgive Ryan. She told him about Bradley and Brooke and how it reminded her of what he and Rhoda went through. Kenneth assured Blake that Ryan fathering a child before they were back together couldn't be compared to him cheating on Rhoda ten years into their marriage. Blake asked him why he did it. Kenneth told her because he could. He explained to Blake that sometimes men do things just because they're able to be done. There's no logic behind it but the rush of how it made him feel fed his ego and the consequences were the last thought in his mind. He told Blake that the woman knew he was married and he was dumb enough to put the life he and Rhoda had built in jeopardy. "I will never tell you I was young, because any man over eighteen cannot use youth as an excuse to abandon their children but I was wrong, irresponsible and a jack donkey for what I did. The way I betrayed your mother is unthinkable and I wasn't man enough to face her or you afterward." said Kenneth. Blake told Kenneth about her assault and it was as if someone shot him in his heart. Shame, regret and anger cloaked him like a cashmere coat. As if he were having an emotional breakdown Kenneth cried like a baby. Blake handed him the box of tissue she had brought with her. For ten minutes Kenneth cried and Blake joined him. The waiter brought water to the table in concern. Kenneth made his way to Blake's side of the table and held her. He apologized for not being there to protect her as rage filled his veins. Blake felt the weight of insecurity leave her body and was grateful Evans had convinced her to go. Over lunch Blake filled Kenneth in on what she had accomplished and Kenneth was happy to see her smile. He told Blake he was happy that Evans treated her like his own. He confided in Blake that not only did Evans beat him down but that Grandpa Rhodes had knocked two of his teeth out with a left hook to the jaw. Blake had heard stories about Grandpa Rhodes and tried not to laugh. Even though she said she wouldn't tell anyone she couldn't wait to tell Rhoda. "Your mother has some men around her who fight first and ask questions later." said Kenneth. Blake agreed. Before parting ways Blake and Kenneth agreed to speak once a month on the third Sunday. She asked if he would walk her out and he told her he didn't want to run into Rocky Balboa. She laughed and left the restaurant 100 pounds lighter.

Josiah and Joelle were having lunch when he told her he was the recipient of a community service award. For the past ten years he had been mentoring young men who were at risk of dying in the streets or being incarcerated. The awards banquet would be held a week later and was a black tie affair. He wanted Joelle by his side and had invited a dozen of his family members from Charlotte. Joelle was excited and hoped that she and Mrs. Carter would have an opportunity to become better acquainted.

Chapter 3: A Secret Struggle

As promised Rose Carter called her and Melvin's family to invite them to Josiah's ceremony. Every time she called a female relative or close friend she decided it was her duty to fill them in on Joelle. There was no use allowing them to form their own opinion of her without knowing who she really was. Rose made it her place to give everyone her opinion before they'd have a chance to meet Joelle. She told the women how Joelle had no formal education and how she came from a broken home. She expressed how good of a man her son was and how he could do better. To the women she knew would understand she expressed how Joelle was very fair and reminded them how "those" women can be. "Men get caught up with these light women and their long hair and all their sense goes out the window." said Rose. Rose used the same mouth she praised the Lord with to spew out venom, judgment and passive aggression toward the woman her son deeply cared for. After three hours of gossip and back biting disguised as prayer requests Rose was exhausted. She told everyone about everyone else and everything she knew about them yet her "sharing" never included herself. You couldn't speak to Rose for fifteen minutes without hearing about Melvin Sr.'s gambling problem or how Josiah suffered from low self-esteem as a child. Never once did Rose think to look in the mirror. Melvin Sr. gambled because she got on his nerves and instead of divorcing her he picked up an outlet for his frustration. He had watched Rose and her religious spirit manipulate people for years. As for Josiah, where would a child get self-esteem when his mother compared him to his deceased brother every day of his life? How would a child know to love himself when he was made to feel inferior to other children? Rose gave Josiah a complex for being dark skinned and for years he didn't know how handsome he really was. The truth is, Rose had no self-esteem and gossiped about others in order to feel good about herself. She was so caught up in her world that she didn't notice that Melvin Sr. had left their marriage emotionally 15 years ago. Rose somehow was able to tell everyone what was wrong with them yet didn't recognize fault in herself. Whenever Rose was approached about the pain or hurt she caused someone she would misuse scripture to justify her actions. Little did Rose Marie Carter know, Joelle Nicole Clarke was time enough for her, she'd already overcome being condemned by her past.

After the Lovehalls returned home after a 10 day stay in Chicago, Nia hadn't returned to work. She had nightmares since the shooting and couldn't sleep at night. A few days before her parents left Nia became friendly with Margot, a stay at home girlfriend to Ethan, an artist, who lived below them on the 14th floor. Nia went to Margot and Ethan's apartment to have someone to talk to since Devin was at work. Margot convinced Nia to have a drink. Willing to try anything to calm her nerves, Nia had four of them. When she returned to her and Devin's home she was able to sleep. Over the next few weeks Nia would drink with Margot while still taking her prescription pills for anxiety. Before long Nia stopped visiting Margot and would drink alone during the day to get some sleep. It was almost thanksgiving and Nia and Devin were scheduled to go to Hampton for the holidays. After a month and a half of her destructive behavior Devin finally realized something was wrong with Nia. The house looked like a tornado hit it and Nia was always in bed. Devin refused to call Parrish or Patricia because he didn't feel like being lectured. Devin called Ryan who was surprised to hear from him since they hadn't spoken since early September. Ryan told Devin his first ministry was his home and he needed to find out what was wrong with Nia. The two men prayed and Devin felt better. As he looked around their house Devin found Nia's stock pile of liquor. He couldn't believe his eyes. He counted 11 bottles of assorted flavored vodka. When he looked in the trash he didn't find any empty bottles. As Devin searched Nia's closet he found 16 empty bottles of liquor. Devin slid down Nia's closet wall and began to cry. How could he have not known? He felt like such a failure. All he was trying to do is maintain the lifestyle Nia was accustomed to but in the process he failed to look after her. He hadn't given himself the opportunity to dwell on the trauma she had suffered because he didn't want to admit he could have lost her to a senseless crime. Devin called a doctor friend to discreetly refer Nia to a wellness center up state. The next morning Devin bathed and dressed his incoherent wife and drove her to the treatment facility a few hours away. When Nia realized where she was she went off! She fought the staff and cussed at Devin blaming him for her condition. "Oh now you want to help me. You're a poor excuse for a husband and I'm telling my daddy!" Devin felt guilty enough without the threat of dealing with Parrish Lovehall. For the next few days Devin stayed at a hotel five minutes from the treatment center and was excused from work because of FMLA. Even though the law protected his leave it was still frowned upon in his profession. Devin knew missing work for a day put his pursuit of partnership in jeopardy let alone the entire month. He made some calls to find another opportunity to work when Nia was better. He was still concerned that Thanksgiving was five days away and Nia's treatment was for 21 days. When Devin arrived at the facility he recognized the woman he married for the first time in weeks. He asked for Nia to cover him as he covered her. She agreed to call her parents and say they weren't coming to thanksgiving in order to spend time alone. The Lovehalls accepted that newlyweds needed time to themselves and excused them from thanksgiving. Devin appreciated his wife's love and Nia appreciated his. She had accepted his apology days prior and promised never to fraternize with Margot.

Weeks later Nia was released from the treatment center and Devin accepted a position to be in-house counsel for a non-profit civil rights organization. He would still make enough money to support them while Nia stayed home and he'd be home every evening by six. In addition to being home at a decent hour Devin could work from home up to five days per month.

As Blake prepared to leave Dr. Agbadou's office she noticed a familiar face. On her desk was a picture of the beautiful bride she had copied her wedding look from. Dr. Agbadou told Blake that was her little sister Ardena. Apparently Ardena was not only a beauty but a celebrated author.Since her talk with Kenneth Blake's perception of Ryan began to change. She recognized that Ryan couldn't be considered a cheater even though Bradley's existence still hurt. Bradley would be spending Thanksgiving with them and Ryan was flying to Dallas to pick him up at the departure gate so he wouldn't have to travel alone. Ryan's plane would land two hours before he and Bradley's flight took off so he'd be at the gate waiting for him. The FAA wouldn't allow Brooke to walk Bradley to the gate but placed him in the care of an agent who would bring him to Ryan. Blake decided she would follow the example of Evans and treat Bradley like she gave birth to him.

For the first time since being a child Apple found her peace. Even though she had to get veneers it was worth telling her mother that she had finally told. Apple decided to pray for Mrs. Brown's healing and deliverance and asked God's forgiveness for disrespecting her mother. She accepted that Ian was the only man who was willing to walk the journey with her and that the men she usually went after didn't feel the same. She had been going to bible study and therapy with Dr. Washington and began to pick up the pieces of her shattered life. She was more present with her children and began to instill values into their young lives. She attended all of Cashmere's recitals, Silk's field trips and picked Chiffon up from daycare on time. Though she didn't know it Apple was beginning to build character and integrity.

Josiah decided not to subject Joelle to Thanksgiving in Charlotte. After his aunts and close friends of his mother looked upon Joelle like a victim at his awards banquet, he needed a break from his mother. Woman after woman offered Joelle prayer for her rough life and encouraged her that God would provide her with the means to an education. Joelle's past was far behind her and under her feet yet Rose made her out to be reprobate. Josiah was beginning to see the woman his mother was. What nerve she had to gossip about Joelle to everyone she knew. She was saddened that Rose felt it necessary to look down on her and attempt to hold her captive to her past. After Josiah shared some personal stories about Rose, Joelle began to feel empathy for her and decided to forgive and move forward.

Laughter could be heard at the Evans home as it was Rhoda and Evans turn to host Thanksgiving. Bradley had fun playing with Beryl and Brice's sons. Evans and Gavin were cracking jokes in his man cave. The women were cooking and eating at the same time and the men were trying to watch a movie in the family room but Grandpa Rhodes was talking smack. He was shocked the night before when Rhoda asked him about knocking Kenneth's teeth out. He told Rhoda it was right after she moved to Maryland after filing for divorce. He saw Kenneth with his mistress at the Stop and Shop and approached him. It was Grandpa Rhodes's testimony that before he could say a word, his arm came to life and punched Kenneth into a cereal display. Rhoda laughed until she cried. She knew her father wasn't right but he sat there with a straight face saying his arm came to life. Because of their growing family Evans had a wall knocked out to expand the formal dining room and had a friend build a custom table. With the exception of the kid's table, the new table was able to seat Evans, Rhoda, Blake, Ryan, Gavin, Victoria, Josh, Rhodes, Lisa, Karen, Beryl, Brice, Vivian and Alex with two seats to spare. Lexi was in Hampton with Paris and Evans mother Beulah was on a cruise.

After a lavish dinner Rhoda served apple pie and pumpkin ice cream for dessert. The entire family piled into the den to watch movies and Ryan almost cried when he noticed Bradley on Blake's lap. He wondered how Devin and Nia were making out but didn't share with anyone that they were having issues. Evans looked around the room and was pleased that things were back on track. That evening everyone slept at the Evans home wherever they found a spot. The following morning the men decided to cook breakfast before everyone left and all agreed to return Saturday evening for leftovers.

During Saturday evening service Blake held Bradley on the front row as Ryan preached his sermon "In All Things Give Thanks". Blake felt another layer of pain leave her spirit during the service. She decided she would walk in love until her intellect caught up with her actions. Ryan was overjoyed to look out at the congregation and see his wife and son. All he wanted was Blake's love and support and now he finally had it. It had been a rough four months but they all had something to be grateful for.

Joelle opened the first progress report on Josette from the Lady of Virtue program. She couldn't believe her eyes when she was informed that Josette had received the top score of 10 in all graded areas of improvement. She was not allowed to speak to her for the first six months of the program but was pleased that her desperate attempt to save Josette may be helping her after all. Johan and Joey were also doing great. Johan was a barber's apprentice and Joelle helped him to get an apartment fifteen minutes away. Joey was still living with Joelle but would stay over Johan's based on his mood. He was attending community college and planned to enter the military after graduation. Josiah got along with Johan and Joey and he made himself available as a male mentor and confidante. He commended Joelle for doing what was right despite it being hard. Josiah had a passion to see the youth make it against the odds and was glad to see the woman he loved care about more than herself.

Brooke was at Granny Mae's getting ready to go to dinner with Jared Mason. Jared was a professional football player whom she met at a joint bachelor/bachelorette party where she was hired to host a stiletto party. Brooke wasn't interested in dating an athlete but after Jared chased her for three months, joined her church and asked Granny Mae if he could take her out she finally agreed. With Bradley out of town with Ryan it was a good opportunity for her to go to dinner without him crossing paths with her son. Brooke decided to wear a black jumpsuit with a leopard clutch and matching booties. She wore her hair in a top knot, wore minimal makeup and her signature Jo Malone fragrance. When Jared pulled up to Granny Mae's house he approached the door with bouquets for both women. Granny Mae smiled as she welcomed Jared inside. Granny loved flowers and was touched by his gesture. As Brook descended the stairs there Jared stood: six foot four, caramel and gorgeous. Brooke acted like she didn't notice how good he looked. She hadn't been in a relationship since Ryan and told Jared straight away that she was not entering into an intimate relationship without marriage. When he told her he understood she agreed to go to dinner. He gave her the flowers he had bought for her and helped her into her emerald green trench coat. They exchanged pleasantries as he opened the door to his automobile and she sat inside. Reaching over to the driver's side she held his door open and he got inside. Together they exchanged general conversation as they made their way to Del Frisco's Double Eagle Steak House.

Minutes later Ryan called Granny Mae's house for Brooke so that Bradley could speak to her. Granny told Ryan that Brooke was out on a date but would tell her to call Bradley the following day due to the time difference. Granny spoke to Bradley and assured him that his mom would call him the next day. As Ryan hung up the phone he found himself wondering who Brooke was with. When Bradley left the room Blake asked where Brooke was. Ryan told her she was on a date. Immediately Blake began to smile and Ryan began to frown.

Chapter 4: Lost

Apple received a call from her sister saying Mrs. Brown was in the hospital. When Apple arrived she found out that her mother had suffered a heart attack. Apple felt terrible because the last time they spoke her mother had punched her. The doctors told Mrs. Brown's children that the attack was massive but they believed she'd pull through.

Several days later Apple returned to the hospital to see her mother. When Mrs. Brown saw Apple she told her she didn't know why she came and to move on as if she were dead. Apple told her mother that she had come to check on her and apologized for the last time they had seen one another. Mrs. Brown told Apple she should be apologizing for lying on Chester and airing her dirty laundry. Apple asked her how she could stick up for Chester when she saw what he and his friend were doing to her. Mrs. Brown told Apple all she saw was her being fast. "Was I fast when Chester came into my room at night when I was only 9 years old?" she asked her mother. "You shut your filthy mouth. You better not repeat that garbage to another person because you probably liked it!" mocked Mrs. Brown. "Why do you like hurting me?" Apple cried. "You hurt me first by being a little dog." said Mrs. Brown. "I'm going to pray for you because I can't allow you to hurt me anymore" said Apple. "Pray for yourself because

I don't need your prayers." scoffed Mrs. Brown. "I love you and I forgive you." said Apple as she kissed her mother on the forehead. "I don't need your forgiveness." Her mother responded. Apple gathered her things and walked out of the hospital.

Moments later Rhoda arrived in Mrs. Brown's room she hadn't seen her in a while but heard about her condition earlier that day through an ex-coworker. Rhoda bought her some flowers and asked how she was doing. She told Rhoda everything was going well except for Apple. When Rhoda asked what was going on Mrs. Brown told Rhoda that Apple had been lying telling people that Chester had molested her as a child. Rhoda told Mrs. Brown that those things aren't something the average person would lie about. She asked Mrs. Brown if she had checked into it. Mrs. Brown told her yes and that there was no proof of Apple's accusations. Rhoda was grieved in her Spirit and knew something was very wrong. She offered to pray for Mrs. Brown and she declined. After a few moments of ministering Rhoda offered Mrs. Brown salvation due to the healing benefits of surrendering her life to Christ, Mrs. Brown declined. Rhoda sat with her old acquaintance catching up and remembering old times on the job. Before Rhoda left she asked Mrs. Brown again if she could pray with her and she declined. She told Mrs. Brown that she really felt the need to lead her to Christ. Mrs. Brown told her she wasn't into all that and declined the invitation. Rhoda backed off after earnestly offering Mrs. Brown the opportunity to have eternal life. She gathered her things, told Mrs. Brown she loved her without reciprocation and left the hospital. Rhoda knew in her heart it would be the last time she saw Mrs. Brown and cried in her car over the bitterness she was willing to carry to her grave. A few hours later Mrs. Brown passed away having denied Jesus Christ.

Mrs. Brown's funeral was modest. There was just enough of a life insurance policy to give her a funeral. Her children were all present including Chester who was released from jail for the funeral. He remained off to the side in prison attire shackled and chained. During the receiving line Rhoda asked one of Mrs. Browns older children why Chester was in jail. She was told that Chester had raped someone. Immediately Rhoda knew Apple was telling the truth. In all her years of knowing Mrs. Brown she never knew Chester was incarcerated. Blake accompanied Rhoda to the funeral and in the receiving line Apple apologized to Blake. Blake told Apple she had forgiven her a long time ago and that it was good to see her. After the funeral Apple made her way over to Chester in the boldness only given through Christ and told him "I remember what you did to me but I forgive you." Rhoda was in ear shot and watched as Chester's head dropped in shame. At that very moment Apple walked away with her head held high and felt empowered and invigorated as never before.

As Nia sat in her weekly AA meeting she was taken by the beauty of his face. She had never seen him before but he stuck out like a sore thumb in a room full of weathered faces. Just then he stood up and spoke "Hi my name is Roy and I'm an alcoholic." The room responded in union with "Hi Roy". He went on to say he began drinking at the age of ten but now at the age of thirty had been sober for two years. After the meeting concluded Roy approached Nia. They exchanged pleasantries and he noticed her fit frame. She told him she worked out in her condo's fitness center four times per week. He offered her his personal training services and handed her his card. Nia was distracted by the feelings that arose within her as he stood before her. She told Roy she would call him never admitting to being married. Devin was in Florida working on a high profile case concerning a young black male who was gunned down for wearing sunglasses at night. Without reservation or hesitation Nia called Roy that night and participated in a four hour conversation agreeing to meet him the following morning in the fitness center of her building.

The next morning Nia showered and dressed in a spandex unitard for her workout session with Roy. When she arrived on the fifth floor he was already waiting for her. The tension between them could be cut with a knife. For forty five minutes Nia completed overtly provocative "exercises" while allowing Roy's hands to sweep across her body in places that should've been reserved for Devin. As if there were no accommodations just feet away Roy asked Nia if he could use her bathroom. With her consent the two of them boarded the elevator for the 15th floor.

After six months of courtship Pastor Elisha agreed to marry Josiah and Joelle. The ceremony would take place in his office with only Lady Nora, Aunt Minnie, Johan and Joey present. Rose refused to come to the wedding in an attempt to stop it and forbade Melvin Sr. from attending. With just a few days to get ready Joelle, Lady Nora and Aunt Minnie went shopping so Joelle could find a winter white suit. The night before the nuptials the six of them gathered to eat dinner at The Water Table when Melvin Sr. arrived. Josiah was so happy to see his father. Melvin apologized for Rose's behavior but said no woman would keep him from his son's wedding. Minnie was so glad Melvin grew a pair. She watched her brother compromise his good sense to be with Rose for years. Deep down she knew Rose was jealous of their relationship because Melvin always confided in her. Rose had a way of acting concerned about others to acquire information only to use it against them later. Minnie was always shocked that Rose was a leader at her church yet tore down the very people she claimed to be assigned to. She knew Rose lived a sheltered life and never had an original thought in her head. Her nephew was happy and that's all that mattered.

The next morning just before noon Joelle became Mrs. Josiah Carter. After an intimate brunch at Simmons restaurant, Joelle and Josiah departed for a honeymoon in Belize.

Another holiday season had come and gone and winter gave way to the spring. Ryan sat on the phone with

Devin who after eleven weeks was about to board a flight back to Chicago. He knew coming home a day earlier than planned would be a good surprise for Nia. The case had been won on behalf of the family of the slain teen and Devin felt on top of the world. In addition to his victory in the courtroom Devin had earned enough money to take a few months off. He told Ryan that he planned to surprise Nia with a trip to Paris. He agreed to stop in Maryland on their way since they hadn't seen each other in months. Ryan suggested that the four of them have a double date like old times. When Ryan hung up Blake asked when they were coming. She hadn't seen her bestie since last August and missed her for not coming home for Thanksgiving or Christmas. Nia had sounded great on the phone for the past month and a half and Blake couldn't wait to catch up.

There were empty bottles of libations all over the bedroom floor. For the past eight weeks Nia and Roy had helped themselves to a Sealy sin fest. Intoxicated with spirits and adultery Nia had become unrecognizable. She flaunted her lover in front of the doorman and neighbors without shame. Openly disrespecting her vows and her temple she gave into her lower nature. The woman who was a virgin on her wedding night had become a drunken harlot. While indulging in ungodly passions and defiling her marriage bed Nia didn't notice the bedroom door swing ajar...

Devin was exhausted as the driver pulled up to the high rise. He was so happy to be home he couldn't contain himself. Just then Gill, the daytime doorman opened his door. Instead of his usual greeting Gill said "Mr. Braxton please alert us if our services are needed." A confused Devin nodded as they each pulled a suitcase from the trunk. When Devin boarded the elevator nausea came upon him without warning. Upon entering his unit he was shocked to see clothes and undergarments laying on the living room floor. Just then he noticed adult DVD cases on his coffee table and his video camera resting on a tripod. Rage arose in Devin for the first time since becoming born again. His breaths became short and heavy as an ecstatic exchange could be heard from inside his bedroom. Praying that his eyes and ears were deceiving him, he opened the door just so. Once he saw Nia engaged in dishonor, Devin blacked out.

Roy pushed Nia off of him as Devin threw the lamp in his direction. Nia became sober at the sight of her day early husband catching her in the act. Roy received the beating of his life as Nia tried to pull Devin off of him. After what seemed like three seconds to Devin and a lifetime to Roy, the fighting ceased. Nia told Devin he would pay for what he did to her man and quickly packed a bag. Roy's blood was all over Devin's shirt and fists as he opened the front door to who he thought were the police banging on it; instead it was the head of the residential board, Seth Levin. He had seen Nia prance around with Roy in Devin's absence and came to diffuse the situation. Seeing it as their opportunity to leave, Roy and Nia headed for the door. As they scurried by Mr. Levin told Nia she would no longer be granted access to the building without a police escort and by two-way radio made sure she and Roy were escorted off the premises. Mr. Levin told Devin he was welcome to the surveillance footage within the building should he ever need it for legal purposes. Devin looked at him with a blank stare as he showed himself the exit. Once alone, Devin rocked back and forth in rage and humiliation. How could the woman he loved entertain another man in his bed? He sacrificed so much in order to make her happy and this was his reward? A typhoon of emotions swept over Devin's mind as he began to cry in a fetal position on the living room floor. After crying himself asleep Devin awoke nine hours later with the headache of his life. He showered and spent time in prayer before calling Ryan to tell him all that had happened.

Ryan was performing a search on the internet of Brooke's new man as he did secretly every week, when the phone rang. Startled as if he'd been caught he closed his laptop before answering the phone. "Whaddup son?" Ryan answered, "We're over." replied Devin. "I caught her in my bed with some dude." Ryan couldn't believe his ears, his cousin Nia was a good girl. For the next hour, Devin sobbed as he told Ryan what went down as Ryan listened in shock with his mouth wide open.

The bass pulsed inside of club Three 6. Apple fist pumped with her left hand while holding a cocktail in her right. She had become friends with a group of women who were in her new convert's class. After searching the bible for the words "thou shall not go to nightclubs" and "thou shall not drink alcohol", they decided it was totally acceptable for a Christian to get their groove on. Apple was quite proud of herself because unlike before when God was watching her children, tonight they were home with Ian. When Apple took a break from dancing to refresh her drink she saw the deaconess from her church who was at her pole dancing class earlier in the week. It was then that she knew for sure that what she was doing was completely acceptable. After pointing out deaconess so and such to the group Apple began to really let loose. Once again she knew something that Blake didn't know; when it comes to being saved, "It doesn't take all of that."

It wasn't until the fourth day of their honeymoon that Joelle realized where she was. If she hadn't been so drunk and high at the time she would have remembered the experience instead of the hotel's name. The Hamanasi resort was not only the backdrop of her new married life but was also the reminder of her old one. As she told Josiah the spotty story of when, why and how she had been there a sense of urgency rose up within her. Anxiety took her over as she began to shake. She may have been unable to remember the details of her exploits in Belize but she knew one thing for sure; she was only two miles away from the $450,000.00 sitting in an account with her name on it.

Nia shook violently as tears fell across her pecan cheeks and into her ears. As she laid on the blow up mattress she and Roy shared in the basement of his Grandparent's home, she read a letter Roy left on the floor. The letter was from the state of Illinois saying they were intercepting Roy's tax return due to unpaid child support. It was just days ago that Roy's grandmother told Nia that Roy had seven children, did not graduate high school and was no more a personal trainer than she was. In actuality Roy had been living with his grandparents since his prison release three months ago and was employed at a local pizza parlor. Nia vomited as she thought about what her parents would think. For weeks she had been lying to them over the phone as if she and Devin were happily married. She was Hampton royalty yet she was living like a pauper. What trust fund baby lives in a basement to keep a man? "He didn't even *know* her." she thought. Though she was ashamed of what she had become and of everything that she had done, she picked up the phone and called Paris.

Less than eight hours after receiving her call Paris arrived in Chicago. He was shocked that his baby sister had been an alcoholic and an adulteress. He felt guilty for not keeping tabs on her after the school shooting and partly blamed himself. He and Lexi were newlyweds too and it surprised him how quickly a marriage can be broken. They hadn't made it to their first anniversary, Paris thought. When he saw Nia outside of the arrival terminal his heart was broken. His beautiful baby sister looked ten years older and was ten pounds too thin.

Across town Ryan and Josh were visiting Devin. They flew to Chicago under the guise of a man trip. Ryan told Blake what had happened but kept Devin and Nia's situation from the family. His parents and his aunt and uncle would've been livid if they knew. A part of Ryan was embarrassed that Nia was his cousin. A part of him felt responsible for not pushing Devin to attend church regularly. Yes you can maintain a relationship with Him anywhere but you are not to forsake the assembly of the saints. Bedside Baptist had claimed the vibrancy of another marriage, Ryan thought.

Joelle shook violently as tears fell across her honey cheeks and into her ears. As she laid across her and Josiah's bed she couldn't believe she had done it. The old Joelle had done some terrible things to acquire those funds but the new Joelle wanted to build a crisis center. Not only did the Holy Spirit tell Joelle to sow all of the $450,000.00, but to sow it anonymously. $200,000.00 was to go to a crisis center she had seen featured on Daystar, $100,000.00 was to be given to Pastor Elisha and Lady Nora, $50,000.00 to the program Josette was in, $50,000.00 to a drug rehabilitation center that once helped her mother and the one seed that was the most difficult to understand, and $50,000.00 as a love gift to Ryan and

Blake. Josiah knew that though hurt Joelle was about to reap a harvest exceeding abundantly above what she could ask or think. He smiled as he held her, she sobbed and shook as she was held.

Paris listened to Nia's confessions as they dined at RPM Steakhouse. He couldn't believe she was capable of such things but knew it was not good the way their parents had sheltered her. It broke his heart to hear her say that though she loved Devin, she married him in order to have sex without condemnation. Nia reminded Paris of the church they grew up in and how Reverend Campbell use to have altar calls for fornication. Paris remembered those altar calls as if it were yesterday. At 16 he remembered the look of disappointment on his Ganny Lovehall's face when he went up to the altar to be "delivered." It was no fun getting called out for a particular sin in front of the congregation but Paris felt it was better to repent from fornication than to enter a Holy covenant with a self-righteous agenda. On one hand he was proud of his baby sister being a virgin on her wedding night just as Lexi was; on the other hand it seemed so deceptive. After their talk Paris promised Nia that Parrish and Patricia would not find out from him. Before Paris could offer advice to Nia he wanted to talk to Devin. Without Nia's permission or consent Paris was meeting Devin later that night at a café in Logan Square.

Meanwhile Ryan, Josh and Devin were having an early dinner at Table Fifty-two. Ryan had finally drummed up the nerve to ask Devin if he was willing to save his marriage. Josh swallowed hard while anticipating Devin's answer. "I don't know." Devin replied. Ryan knew Devin was meeting with his cousin Paris and wondered what Paris's position was on the matter. "Would you have saved your marriage if it happened to you?" Devin inquired. "I've been thinking that very thing all day and like you, I don't know. I do know one thing for sure, I would want to be forgiven." said Ryan. "I need to be forgiven right now." said Ryan. "What for?" asked Josh. "For being wildly jealous that Brooke has a man." After Ryan's admission, the three of them sat in silence for the remainder of their meal then returned to Devin's condo to relax.

Later that evening Devin sat in a small café waiting for Paris to arrive. His stomach was in knots and he felt vulnerable and embarrassed. When Paris walked in and saw his brother-in-law his heart broke. Just like Nia, Devin was the victim of rapid and unhealthy weight loss. As Devin stood up to greet him Paris embraced him. They both began to cry. Patrons assumed they were in a relationship. "I'm sorry." Paris sobbed, "I'm sorry too." Devin responded. The two brothers sat for hours discussing Nia's behavior, Devin's pressure to provide and his fear of Parrish. Paris knew his father was hard on Devin and Texan and he apologized on his behalf. He knew his father's shoes were big shoes to fill and was glad that Quinn and Nia were his sisters and not his love interests. Before departing Paris asked if Devin was willing to save his marriage and like he told Ryan he told Paris. He respected Devin's answer because he didn't know if he could forgive Lexi of the same thing.

When Devin arrived at home Ryan told him that his uncle Parrish had called three times because he saw the call come across the television screen. Devin checked his messages but Parrish didn't leave one. Earlier that evening Nia decided to tell her parents the truth because she was tired of lying. Devin's heart raced as he returned the call to Parrish's cell phone. "Hello son." Parrish answered. "Hey Dad." Devin responded. "Baby girl told me everything and before you say anything I just want you to know I don't take her deeds lightly. She has broken my heart and sullied my family name. I know you have a lot to think about and a lot to determine but I have a proposition for you. If you take her back I will give you three million dollars immediately and half of her inheritance upon my death." Devin couldn't believe his ears. "I don't know dad." Devin said softly. "Okay let me sweeten the pot. In addition to the three million, a new car every five years and I'll build you two a home wherever you want to live." Parrish added. Patricia overheard their conversation and though it was unseemly she hoped Devin would comply. Parrish told Devin he had 72 hours to accept and hung up the phone.

When Devin told Ryan what his uncle proposed he shook his head. He told Devin it was his choice and he would support him either way. Josh and Ryan had heard

Gavin tell stories about Parrish buying Patricia from Pop Pop by paying all his debts and building him and Mumzie a house but they always thought their father was joking. Parrish really thought having money meant never saying you're sorry.

Chapter 5: Disorderly Conduct

Blake was excited that Ryan was on his way home. Nia wouldn't answer her calls and she couldn't wait to hear what really happened in Chicago. She forgot to tell Ryan that a giving initiative had sent them a cashier's check for $50,000.00 on behalf of an anonymous donor. Blake knew that she and Ryan had helped countless people so she wasn't going to waste her time trying to figure out who sent it. It was received just five days after they gave $10,000.00 out of their personal money to dig two wells in a village in South America. God's economic system beat Wall Street every day of the week. Since it was a beautiful spring day she decided to get a Panini and lemonade at a small bistro in Columbia. As Blake sat in a window seat eating and reading on her I pad, she was approached by Joelle. Blake was surprised to see her and they hadn't crossed paths since Joelle's debut sermon almost a year prior. Joelle asked if she could join her and Blake accepted. They laughed when they realized that they ordered the same meal including extra pesto mayo on the side and no onion. "I was hoping we'd run into each other." said Joelle. "I need to apologize to you for the way I handled everything. I thought you were a weak momma's girl who knew nothing about real life. I didn't consider you on my level and somehow felt superior to you. You and momma Ro were nothing but kind to me and the only family I had and I ruined it. Please forgive me." Blake was heartbroken by Joelle's words because she didn't know Joelle thought those things about her. She told Joelle that it hurts her that she felt that way but that she forgives her completely. Blake apologized for walking in offense when Joelle lived at their house. Joelle accepted her apology. After an identical lunch and mutual forgiveness they departed not to be enemies nor to be friends, just two women who wished the other God's best.

After two months of clubbing every weekend Apple stopped going to church. She was always too tired or too hung over to attend. What bothered her the most was that Ian and the children continued to go and every week the children asked why they had to go if mom didn't. Apple was ashamed and accused Ian of judging her when he told the children not going was between mom and the Lord. His bible told him that by their fruits you shall know them and he wasn't being her judge just her fruit inspector. Apple began to resist Ian's headship and authority leaving their home wide open to the enemy. Through his married mentor's tutelage Ian decided to fight for their broken marriage. In a desperate attempt to bring stability into their home Ian had been financing Apple's dreams. Six months ago Apple announced she wanted to be a caterer so Ian sent her to food safety classes and rented her a spot in a commercial kitchen. After three weeks of selling meals, Apple announced she wanted to be a realtor like Sister Parker after seeing she drove a Range Rover. After two classes she told Ian that the curriculum was too challenging because there was too much to remember and dropped out. Three months ago she wanted to be a makeup artist because she remembered how successful Joelle had been in beauty. A local cosmetic boutique allowed her to freelance but she soon found out that everyone with a set of brushes, isn't a makeup artist. Her clients looked like clowns and so did she. One month ago after watching David Tutera she decided her passion was to be a wedding planner. Ian had the business cards printed and added another phone line for her clients. Now after another desperate attempt to fill the God hole Apple told Ian she wanted to be a daycare provider.

As Devin sat alone pondering Parrish's proposition, he realized that he hadn't spoken to his parents since the night before he left Florida. He and his siblings were raised to be independent and it wasn't unusual to only check in once or twice per month. Drs. Harold and Joni Braxton couldn't believe their ears. When Devin told them what Parrish proposed, they were appalled. Their son was not for sale and neither were his morals. While speaking to his parents Devin realized he knew the answer all along. Devin assured his parents he wasn't taking Nia back because though he loved her he also loved himself. The next morning Devin filed for divorce citing infidelity as the cause.

Gavin, Victoria and Blake were speechless when Ryan and Josh filled them in on their man trip to Chicago.

Gavin was disappointed in his niece but wasn't surprised about the money. Though he knew Parrish was that kind of man, he prayed that his sister Patricia wasn't that kind of woman. Blake's heart broke for Nia so she decided to call. Nia answered the phone and immediately told Blake she didn't know what to say. Blake told Nia that she loved her, was still her best friend and was there to hold her hand through the storm. Nia was so relieved to have a true friend in Blake. As they spent the next few hours talking Nia told Blake everything.

That night in bed Blake was thankful that Nia gave her the opportunity to be a friend during her night season. Joelle had once robbed her of true friendship and it felt good to love someone back to life. Ryan was impressed with how far Blake had come and he appreciated her capacity to love.

Joelle's heart raced as Dr. Smith walked into the room. She had Joelle's test results. For years Joelle had unprotected sex and didn't get pregnant. She didn't think anything of it until she married Josiah. Dr. Smith told Joelle that due to Pelvic Inflammatory Disease she was unable to have children. Joelle was crushed. All the years of living recklessly, acquiring STD's and not knowing to value her body had taken its toll. She sobbed as Dr. Smith held her in compassion. After gathering her composure Joelle gathered her things and headed to her car. As she sat in the car in silence Josiah called to check on her. She told him the results of the test. Though his heart broke he told Joelle they served Jehovah Rapha and that by the stripes of Jesus Christ she was healed. Joelle gained strength from his words and began the drive home.

Josiah was processing what Joelle had told him when Melvin called. In a moment of humanity and trust Josiah confided in his father that Joelle was unable to have children. His father comforted him the best he could since he wasn't a very spiritual man. He told his son that he had his confidence and he would talk to him soon. When Josiah hung up his spirit was troubled so he decided to cook dinner for himself and Joelle so they could have a peaceful night.

When Rose realized Melvin was talking to Josiah she asked how he was doing. Melvin told her that their son was hurting because his wife couldn't have children. Rose couldn't believe her ears. Miss cutie on duty couldn't have children! Before an hour went by Rose had called all of her "prayer partners" to tell them the news. By the next day she had told Josiah's third grade teacher when she ran into her at CVS and his sixth grade bully's mother when she saw her at Harris Teeter. Rose wasn't convicted in any way for uncovering her family and tearing down her son in the process.

Later that week when Josiah logged onto his e-mail he had an inbox from Mrs. Banks his third grade teacher. She told him she was praying for him and Joelle and that the Drs. told her she couldn't conceive and her and her husband had five children. Josiah was crushed. Rose had gone too far this time. He knew not to trust Melvin with his heart but he caught him at a weak moment. It was then that Josiah vowed not to tell his parents anything he wouldn't tell a complete stranger. The scriptures do command that you honor your parents but in turn God asks them not to provoke their children to wrath. Josiah told Joelle that he confided in Melvin who after saying it was confidential told his mother who told the world. Joelle didn't expect much from Rose and knew she was a bitter woman who hid behind a religious spirit and forgave her husband instantly.

Twins Lebron and Carmelo couldn't be comforted. Apple paced the floor with them trying to soothe their cries. To make matters worse she was going to have to explain to Ty'Quessha how Prada was able to cut two of her ponytails off. These children were getting on her last nerves. Thank goodness Ian's grandmother kept Chiffon so she didn't have to put up with her. It was nap time yet only Barak was asleep. Apple couldn't wait for the school bus to drop off Jezebel from a.m. kindergarten because though she was only five, she had a way of keeping the other kids under control.

Blake was exceptionally cheerful while walking down the hall of the hospital. Each month she would do outreach with a different ministry at the church and today she joined the intercessory team. Rhoda was the head of the ministry and had become quite the prayer warrior as

God prepared her for the mantle. Each time the team arrived at the hospital they were given a list of patients who wanted prayer. Blake was on her way to room 911 to pray for Ms. Smith, a woman who was listed as having suffered broken legs and arms in a car accident. As Blake walked to the room she felt the anointing fall on her in a way that hadn't happened before. Knocking on the open door Blake asked "Ms. Smith are you decent? I'm here to pray with you. Come in." an eerie voice answered. Blake walked into the room and saw Cabria laying on the bed. When Cabria saw Blake she couldn't believe her eyes. Something was different about her. She was beautiful, well dressed and silently powerful. Her appearance immediately made Cabria insecure. "Hello There." said Blake. "Hi." Cabria replied. Without malice, revenge or hate but in the possession of pure love, Blake prayed for the woman who had caused her such pain and harm, that she surprised herself. After small talk and well wishes Blake walked out of room 911 and headed to room 316 all the while knowing, that God was so real.

Devin was re-writing his five year plan when Mr. Levin knocked on his door. When Devin answered he was told there was a package for him downstairs that needed to be signed for. When he stepped off the elevator and entered the lobby a casually dressed man resembling Larry the Cable Guy handed him a clipboard and asked him to sign. Devin was confused because he hadn't ordered anything. Just then the man handed him the keys to a brand new Indium Grey Metallic G550 Mercedes

SUV. Devin knew it was a gift from Parrish who he had told over two weeks ago that he was not taking Nia back under no circumstances. Devin told the driver to put the truck back on the carrier and return it to sender. The truck driver told Devin he was in the delivery business not the return business. After parking the car in the garage to get it off the street Devin called Parrish. "She's pretty ain't she son?" he answered the phone. "I can't keep it because I'm not taking her back." said Devin. "You have to come get it." "She ain't mine boy. Just like my daughter, I gave her to you." said Parrish. "Well I can't keep her or your daughter." added Devin. "Sure you will keep them both. Besides, the title and Illinois registration are in your name just like my daughter, she's a Braxton." Parrish hung up. When Patricia asked him how it went he replied "everyone has a price we just haven't found his." Devin went back up to his condo and found a company that would ship the truck back to Virginia.

Nia was sitting on the bed in her childhood bedroom when Patricia knocked on her door. She had moved back home since being served with Devin's divorce filing while leaving an AA meeting. When her mother walked in she told Nia that Devin was still unwilling to take her back after receiving the truck. Nia was shocked because it was his dream car in his dream color. She knew it wasn't ideal to buy her husband back but she knew it wasn't a good look to come home just months after being married, especially in Hampton. She had been raised to care about appearances. She and Quinn knew the importance of being a Lovehall. Paris was the only one who bucked against the system. He was angry with Nia for playing their parents' game and assured his baby sister that the worse kind of man to be married to, is the man who doesn't want you. Deep down Nia knew it was true but she was content with living a lie. Besides, women did it all the time. There's the women who gave their man an ultimatum to get married, the women who got pregnant to keep him, the women who won their man by default, the women who let him have other women, the women willing to always be his fiancée and Nia was willing to be the kind who paid him to stay.

Chapter 6: If It's Not One Thing

Joelle was having a bad day. Everything seemed to go awry. After getting fully dressed her pants split on her way out the door. Once back upstairs she changed from a pant suit to a skirt suit and when she got in her car her pantyhose ran. Having no more hosiery in the same color, she stopped at Walgreens to pick up a quick pair and her car was hit in the parking lot. After exchanging insurance information she was late to her meeting and began to rush. While rushing she was pulled over by the police and was given a speeding ticket. Now officially late, she called the hostess of the meeting and told her she was running late after a fender bender and being pulled over for speeding. The hostess told Joelle that she forgot to tell her the day before that the meeting was cancelled. Joelle was heated! She still had two hours before a meeting with Lady Nora for the annual women's conference so she stopped to get something to eat. While waiting for her food, someone knocked her drink over with their briefcase while squeezing by her table staining her light pink suit. After eating lunch she got into her car to drive home so she could change clothes. As she pulled out of the parking lot of the café she realized she had a flat tire. Wanting to crawl back in bed and start the day over, she called Josiah to vent while she waited for AAA but his assistant told her he was in a meeting. Finally she made it home only to find that the hot water tank had burst. Annoyed that she was running late again she headed to Pastor Elisha and Lady Nora's house after deciding it would have to wait. Once she reached her destination she tried to put on a happy face. Marisol, the house keeper escorted her to the sitting room where Lady Nora sat speaking to Evangelist Booth. Upon arrival the ladies could tell that Joelle had pressed her way. As Joelle began to calm her nerves the other speakers trickled into the room. After a two hour conversation on the vision and theme of the conference Lady Nora dismissed the meeting and offered the women an early dinner in the formal dining room. As they were heading to freshen up before dinner Joelle was stopped by Evangelist Booth. Over the course of the afternoon Joelle learned that though originally from Maryland, she had flown in from Columbus, Ohio for Lady Nora's meeting. She was a graduate of Valor Christian College and a true woman of God. After allowing all the women to leave the room Evangelist Booth asked Joelle if she could pray for her. Joelle agreed. Before she knew it she was on her back as the spirit of infirmity was cast out of her. By the Spirit Evangelist Booth proclaimed complete restoration of Joelle's reproductive system and declared that three healthy children would be born from her womb in the name of the Lord. She commanded the unclean spirit to leave through the door it entered into and shut the door on its way out. She applied the Blood of Jesus to the door then placed an angel at the door in prayer. Joelle was so grateful, she had never heard anyone pray that way before. She literally felt the release in her physical body and began to praise God. She hugged Evangelist Booth's neck and wouldn't let her go. The commotion had caught the attention of Pastor Elisha who rejoiced with them.

After a wonderful dinner of orzo and shrimp salad, stuffed cod, asparagus and ginger peach tea the ladies exchanged either phone numbers or well wishes. Lady Nora gave them gift bags full of body care products and pajamas as they left. After speaking one last time to Evangelist Booth, Joelle got into her car. She noticed Josiah had called her three times and she was about to return his call when one of the ladies knocked on her window. The woman was a Pastor's wife from a church in Colorado who hadn't spoken much during dinner. Joelle smiled as she opened the window. The woman's name was Lynn. Lynn told her she knew all afternoon that Joelle was her real assignment and not the meeting. She said it was unheard of to fly so far for the planning stages of an upcoming conference but Nora and Elisha have been good friends with her and her husband so she came. She told Joelle as soon as she saw her she knew why she had come. "God told me weeks ago to prepare this check and to keep it with me and he would show me who to give it to. He told me you needed it to open a crises center for women so please receive this." said Lynn. "I receive" Joelle replied. Lynn walked to the town car waiting for her, slid inside and rode away. As Joelle unfolded the check for $1,500,000.00, all she could do was cry.

As Ryan sat in his office studying for Sunday's message, the phone rang. Not recognizing the name or number he answered. "Daddy can you come and get me?" Bradley cried. "What's wrong?" Ryan quizzed. "Jared sent me in a cab to Granny Mae's house and she's not home" Bradley answered. "Why would he put you in a cab? Where's your mother?" Ryan exclaimed. "I'm at Jared's house. She said I was getting on his nerves so I had to go." Bradley cried. "Where are you calling me from?" Ryan quizzed. "Miss Karla's house next door to Granny Mae." Bradley answered. Ryan tried to keep his composure as he told Bradley to put Miss Karla on the phone. Miss Karla told Ryan that Granny Mae had been in the hospital for three days and Brooke hasn't returned anyone's calls or come by. She went on to tell Ryan that Brooke has changed for the worse since hooking up with Jared and has become quite the party girl. Ryan asks Miss Karla if she could keep Bradley until he flew to Texas and she agreed. Ryan's blood began to boil as he left the church and called Blake to meet him at BWI.

In an effort to cheer Nia up Patricia decided to buy her a new spring and summer wardrobe. Never one to be outdone she called in stylist and personal shopper extraordinaire Kayla Laurén. While at the Lovehall estate Kayla edited Nia's closet and brought in over $20k worth of clothing and accessories. Nia sat on the floor of her massive walk-in closet as Kayla grouped the clothes together in looks for her to try. Patricia was amazed how down she still was after seeing all the fabulous clothes.

When Nia stepped into a Trina Turk maxi dress with Tori Burch sandals Patricia's eyes light up. Oh Nia that's a find me a new man outfit! Patricia exclaimed. Just then Kayla looked up from the racks and said in a matter of fact tone, "Remember the treasure doesn't do the hunting." After an "I know that's right!" from Patricia, they shared a high five as Nia stood in front of them with her secret shame... She was pregnant with Roy's baby.

As Apple sifted through her mail she came across a thick grey envelope addressed to her. As she opened it she noticed it was from her sister Gloria. Wondering why her sister would mail her something instead of calling Apple rushed to empty its contents. Attached to the documents was a post-it note that read, *I hope this gives you peace after all she put you through.* Apple unfolded the documents and couldn't believe her eyes. Contained in the envelope were her adoption papers. After reading the pages that followed Apple learned that she was conceived by her father and his under aged mistress. When she was six months old, an open adoption was made from her sixteen year old mother to Mrs. Gertrude Brown. When Apple did the math her father was 37 at the time. On one hand she was relieved that Mrs. Brown wasn't her biological mother and on the other hand she was ashamed that her father got a teen pregnant while married. Her mother was listed as Christina Marie Jackson. Knowing that she needed support and the courage to begin again, Apple called Dr. Washington.

Devin had finally sold his condo and moved into a townhouse in Highland Park. He was glad to get away from the reminder of Nia's affair and was happy to change all of his contact information. Parrish had done everything in his wallet's power to get him to take her back. The last straw was when Michael Jordan's assistant called to confirm their one on one game of basketball. Nia knew MJ was his hero and he resented her for playing with his dreams and emotions. After a chance run-in with a client who was also in Nia's AA group, Devin learned that Roy had shared with the group that Nia was pregnant. He went as far as telling them that she used him for his body and caused him to fall off the wagon before running back to Virginia. Devin kept the information to himself and waited for the day that Ryan would confirm it.

As the Carters left a meeting with the board members they'd appointed for the crisis center, Joelle was served. When they got into the car she opened the subpoena. She was called to be a witness against Tevin for bank and insurance fraud and if she declined would face indictment. After weathering so many storms with God by her side, Joelle knew not to fret. To whom much is given much is required and she knew that though the weapons had formed, they surely wouldn't prosper.

It was a mild Friday night when Ryan and Blake landed at Dallas Fort Worth airport. Trying to remain calm they drove their rented car to Miss Karla's house.

Upon arrival Ryan noticed Brooke's car parked in Granny Mae's driveway. As Ryan knocked on Karla's door, Brooke busted out of Granny Mae's door in a drunken stupor. "Awww shucks! Reverend Ryan wants to be a daddy now and come to his baby's rescue! Where were you when he needed pampers and diapers man of gawd?" as Brooke fumbled her words. Miss Karla welcomed the Hairstons in as Brooke began to bang on her door. Bradley had fallen asleep in a recliner as he waited on his father. Ryan woke him up and held him as he began to cry. Bradley was startled when he heard Brooke outside the door yelling. Ryan thanked Karla, gave her a few bills and made his way out the door and past Brooke. "You're always embarrassing me when you get drunk." Bradley cried. "Oh shut up Pastor's boy, you think you're better than everybody." Ryan belted Bradley in the car before approaching Brooke. "What's going on with you Brooke? You're one of the best mothers I've ever met. I'm getting my life Rev-r-ent. I'm taking him back to Maryland with me. Go head passa...You're meeting me at a lawyer's office tomorrow to have papers drawn up. Okay man-a-gawd. You gotta take him anyway cause I'm about to be on tv." said Brooke with her eyes glossed over. Ryan was beyond annoyed. He took Bradley and Brooke and checked into the Omni hotel.

The following morning Ryan, Blake and Bradley went to visit Granny Mae at Baylor University Medical Center. After assuring Bradley that she was fine, Granny Mae asked Blake to take Bradley to get a snack. While alone with Ryan, Granny Mae told him that she was terminally ill. She said that Brooke refused to come see her because she couldn't handle what was happening. Granny asked Ryan to promise not only to take care of Bradley but to make sure that Brooke wasn't left by the way side. Ryan promised and proceeded to pray for Granny Mae. Once they left the hospital they met Brooke at an attorney's office to give Ryan primary custody of Bradley. Blake was amazed how well Brooke looked and sounded after being a total wreck just hours prior. She sat across the table in a cream Lanvin peplum dress and Christian Louboutin Malabar Hill pumps. Blake had to admit Brooke was the epitome of style and her shoe game was second to none. Before they left, Brooke told Bradley she'd come to visit and he told her she was a liar. He told Brooke she likes Jared better than him and he was never coming back. Brooke ignored his statement and told Bradley he would soon be able to see her on television.

Apple maintained her silence as she sat across from a disappointed Dr. Washington at lunch. Lovingly but firmly she told Apple it was time to grow up and get her act together. Dr. Washington asked her why Ian and the children were attending worship service alone and why she stopped coming to therapy when she was kind enough to render her services for free. Apple immediately felt ashamed. Dr. Washington waited for an answer and stared Apple directly in her eyes saying nothing...

"I don't know." said Apple as if she were four. "Are you kidding me?" Dr. Washington replied. "You expect me to believe that a 29 year old woman with a husband, children and the life experiences of someone three times your age doesn't know why you don't value others?" Dr. Washington added. "Yes." said Apple. "Let me help you dear, you don't value yourself. You've given your all to people who cared nothing for you yet Ian and I receive your abuse of our love. "You're a glutton for punishment but starved for love." Dr. Washington preached. "I don't know how to receive love." Apple exclaimed. Dr. Washington explained to Apple that she wouldn't learn how to give and receive love until she had a genuine relationship with the Father. She told Apple she was no longer a helpless child in the basement but has the tools at her fingertips to become a woman of integrity who can learn to love herself. "I have an assignment for you." said Dr. Washington as he wrote on a piece of paper and handed it to Apple:

Rededicate your life back to the Lord

Return to therapy

Volunteer

"Why do I have to volunteer?" Apple questioned. "Because you haven't begun to live until you make a difference in the lives of others." said Dr. Washington. "I'm sending you to a women's crisis center where I sit on the board of directors. I'm giving you another chance to prove me right. What are your catering hours?" the Dr. asked. "I don't cater anymore." said Apple. "Right you switched to real estate." said Dr. Washington. "Not that either." Apple said embarrassed. "Then what?" said Dr. Washington as she was losing her patience. "After real estate I was a makeup artist, then a wedding planner, then a daycare provider but I'm starting class soon to become a phlebotomist." explained Apple. Dr. Washington looked at Apple with a blank stare. "A jack of all trades huh? Do you realize you're exemplifying the symptoms of a victim? Long ago someone stole your identity and all these years later you're searching for yourself. Before you become a phlebotomist I'd like you to spend a season seeking God for His purpose for your life." as Dr. Washington ministered to Apple. "How?" Apple inquired. "In your prayer time before the Lord." said Dr. Washington "What's a season?" Apple quizzed. "Around ninety days." said Dr. Washington with compassion in his eyes. She knew Apple had been clubbing and drinking but knew her behavior wouldn't change until her belief system did. Just before leaving Dr. Washington handed Apple the card to the Beauty for Ashes Crisis Center for Women. Apple's eyes light up when she saw the name of its founder Mrs. Joelle Carter.

Parrish was livid when he found the ultrasound pictures of Nia's baby in her glove box. He had bought her car to the dealership to have it detailed. He immediately called Patricia who first got excited. "Devin will have no choice but to take her back now." she exclaimed. "Pat, could you please use your head for anything other than a mounting post for that expensive hair? That baby doesn't belong to Devin it belongs to that thug she met in AA." Patricia immediately became enraged. She barged through Nia's bedroom door in a whirlwind. "Please tell me you're not knocked up by that broke looser you cheated with!" she yelled. "Who are you and where is my daughter? We don't get pregnant by hoods and thugs. If by chance we did have a temporary lapse in judgment we'd dispose of the evidence." Patricia fumed. "I'm keeping it!" Nia yelled with tears in her eyes. "Like hades you are! You want everyone to know you lay with dogs?" Patricia taunted. "My baby is innocent and I am keeping her. Blake said she would help me." Nia cried. "Oh but sweetheart Blake doesn't have to bear the humiliation of having played in the trash! Get rid of it or get out." Patricia slammed the door behind her as she put the receiver back up to her ear. "Parrish did you hear what your daughter said?" Patricia cried. "Pat the question is, did she hear what you said?" Parrish answered.

Nia knew that her father shared her mother's sentiments. She also knew that Quinn was their robot and would never support her decision to keep her baby. Nia picked up her phone and called the only one who loved her unconditionally, her brother Paris.

Paris was deeply hurt when his baby sister told him of her plight. He knew his parents well enough to know that they couldn't see past how Nia's pregnancy made *them* look. As he did in Chicago Paris offered Nia his love and support. Though he wanted more for her, the consequences of her decisions had outrun his wishes. With Lexi's consent he offered Nia a place to stay until she devised a plan B for the future of herself and his niece.

After putting Bradley to bed Ryan and Blake settled in the family room to watch their favorite forensic drama. As if it weren't enough on their plates to make Bradley's transition a smooth one, there it was: an extended trailer of an upcoming reality show "Football Fiancés" starring Brooke Taylor and four other women casually linked to professional athletes. With mouths wide open they watched as Brooke turned over tables, smashed a car window, fought in a department store and cursed like a sailor. To add insult to injury Brooke stated that she was the fiancée of Jared Mason but has a child with Maryland pastor Ryan Hairston. She went on to say that Ryan abandoned her and their son to marry his mistress and now wife, Lady Blake Hairston.

Immediately their cell and house phones began to ring. For the following hour Ryan and Blake received calls from a dozen people vowing their support and expressing their disgust. None more than momma Rhoda who said things that couldn't be repeated. Ryan called Devin for legal advice. Devin told Ryan a cease and desist letter could be served to the show as well as slander and defamation filings.

That night Ryan had the distinct misfortune of deciding whether to take legal action against the mother of his child. He knew it would take much prayer and wise counsel to decide what he should do. Not only would this affect his family but the flock that God had entrusted to him. He immediately thought of the promise he made to Granny Mae and the words of Joyce Meyer: "As many people as you can help is also the same number of people you can hurt." Ryan knew this was an attack of the enemy but he also knew he served a mighty God. Instead of toiling in his flesh he chose to fall on his face and pray.

In a neighboring city Joelle went into prayer for Ryan and Blake after viewing the Football Fiancés trailer. She had no idea that Ryan had a son and didn't know the circumstances. She did know that Blake wouldn't be anyone's mistress and could vouch for their integrity both in and outside of the church. They were all under the headship of Pastor Elisha and at the end of the day Joelle knew that made them family.

Across town Apple became excited after seeing the trailer for Football Fiancés. "Finally Blake would have to admit she isn't all that." Apple thought. Little did she know Bradley wasn't a dirty little secret, nor would Blake crumble under the pressure. God gave her the grace to handle her and Ryan's calling and God never abandons what He births. Apple was like so many people who believed in order for them to win, you had to lose. Her lowly mindset was just another example of not knowing who *she* was.

As Blake sat in her home office she was fatigued. She knew she needed to take a break after all she had before her. Blake decided to check her calendar in order to choose a date for the spa. While looking through her itinerary it was flooded with meetings to get her new project off the ground. Blake was establishing a nonprofit organization to partner inner city girls with mentors who had become successful despite their circumstances. She would start with ten girls from the ages of 10-18 who based on similar goals would be mentored by women in diverse professions. The mentors included a magazine publisher, a judge, a surgeon, an attorney, a chef, a motivational speaker, an investor, a fashion designer, a pilot and a professor. All the women were handpicked by Blake and Rhoda after meeting a strict list of qualifying requirements. In addition to the mentoring program Blake was working on an annual award gala to honor women of excellence. She called the honor the Light Award founded on Matthew 5:16 and Romans 13:7. After working for the past two years to bring her vision to fruition, Blake tirelessly sought women across the country who did their deeds to God's glory not seeking honor for themselves. Women of character and distinction who would go otherwise unsung and uncelebrated. Three of the five women for next year's ceremony were already chosen but not yet informed. They were philanthropist Lela Campbell, sixth grade educator Bella Scott and local circuit court judge and a mentor in her organization, Christina Marie Jackson. All her thoughts came screeching to a halt when Blake's calendar revealed that her cycle was a week overdue.

Joelle's assistant Rema knocked on her office door and told her that her new volunteer had arrived. A nauseated Joelle told Rema to send her inside. Just then Apple came prancing into Joelle's office offering a "Hey girl!" from her lips. Annoyed by her arrogance and false sense of familiarity Joelle replied "My name is Mrs. Carter." Apple knew by Joelle's expression that she meant business and immediately grew embarrassed. Normally Apple would've stormed out after telling the person off but she knew Dr. Washington's name and trust were on the line. Without pleasantries Joelle stated the vision and mission of opening Beauty for Ashes. Apple shifted in her seat as Joelle spoke. Dressed in a red peplum suit with her cut in an asymmetrical feathered bob, a beat faced Joelle sat in silence. Apple had been caught with her mind wandering and asked Joelle if she could repeat the question. Joelle visibly annoyed asked a second time if Apple understood the responsibilities of being a volunteer. Apple answered yes and asked who she'd be counseling and Joelle told her the shelves of the food pantry. Apple was about to pop off when she decided to remain calm and accept the terms of Joelle's proposal. Because she had small children Joelle decided to allow Apple to volunteer on Tuesday,

Wednesday and Thursday from 10am-2pm. She told Apple she would be required to be on time, stay the entire shift and work on all scheduled days. Apple wasn't big on being punctual but she agreed. As Joelle sat behind her desk Apple decided she wanted to be like her: confident, strong and beautiful. Though she knew she needed Joelle's mentorship Apple was too proud to ask and decided to watch her instead.

Later that evening Blake and Joelle sat on the edge of their tubs over twenty miles apart. Blake in her on suite and Joelle in her bathroom, waited in optimism and expectation. Ryan and Josiah each with their wife thought how their lives would change if the results were positive. With the weight of ministry and pending court cases both couples would be bringing children into the world at the busiest times of their lives. No longer friends but connected on a much higher level than they'd admit, Blake and Joelle were excited at the idea of pregnancy and motherhood. Just like synchronized swimmers Ryan and Josiah read the results of the first response pregnancy tests.

57871267R00060

Made in the USA
Charleston, SC
24 June 2016